"My sister told me that once you knew about Cody being your son, you'd help keep him safe."

"Why have you decided to spring this news on me now?" Alex asked.

He glanced at Shelby's upset expression, feeling an uncharacteristic flash of sympathy for her. *Don't go there,* he warned himself. He'd help Cody and Shelby but becoming emotionally involved was out of the question.

"Because Cody's in danger. Early this morning my sister called and asked me to meet her down at the marina. Trina asked me to take Cody and made me promise to keep him safe. On the way to my car, Trina spotted someone. She told me to run and she took off, heading back toward the marina. I caught a glimpse of a man with a gun. I—I grabbed Cody and ran."

"And Trina?" Alex forced himself to ask.

"I think he killed her." Shelby's voice was barely above a whisper. "She risked her life to save us. She drew the gunman away, sacrificing herself to save her son. Your son."

Books by Laura Scott

Love Inspired Suspense

The Thanksgiving Target
Secret Agent Father

LAURA SCOTT

grew up reading faith-based romance books by Grace Livingston Hill, but as much as she loved the stories, she longed for a bit more mystery and suspense. She is honored to write for the Love Inspired Suspense line at Steeple Hill Books, where a reader can find a heartwarming journey of faith amid the thrilling danger.

Laura lives with her husband of twenty-five years and has two children, a daughter and a son, who are both in college. She works as a critical-care nurse during the day at a large level-one trauma center in Milwaukee, Wisconsin, and spends her spare time writing romance.

Please visit Laura at www.laurascottbooks.com as she loves to hear from her readers.

Secret Agent Father

Laura Scott

Steeple
Hill®

Published by Steeple Hill Books™

STEEPLE HILL BOOKS

Steeple
Hill®

Recycling programs
for this product may
not exist in your area.

ISBN-13: 978-0-373-44394-9

SECRET AGENT FATHER

Copyright © 2010 by Laura Iding

www.SteepleHill.com

Printed in U.S.A.

So we say with confidence,
"The Lord is my helper; I will not be afraid.
What can man do to me?"
—*Hebrews* 13:6

This book is dedicated to my sister Joan,
thanks for reading my books. I love you!

ONE

"I made a terrible mistake," her sister Trina said in a low voice, her expression bleak. "I need you to take Cody."

Shelby Jacobson shivered from the desperation in her sister's tone as much as the sharp March wind blowing off the rocky shores of Lake Michigan. Her gaze fell upon her four-and-a-half-year-old nephew, huddled with Trina. Beneath the hood of Cody's coat, his bright green eyes were wide and frightened within his pale face.

Instinctively she knelt down before him, holding out her arms. Cody broke away from his mother, flinging himself at Shelby, burying his face against her chest. She crushed him close, frowning at Trina over his head.

"Of course I'll take him. But why? What's going on? Why did you drag me out of bed and ask me to come down to the marina at four-thirty in the morning?"

Trina didn't flinch under her glare, but Shelby saw a flash of unmistakable regret flicker across her sister's eyes. Trina thrust a piece of paper into Shelby's hand, along with a cell phone. "Here. When you get to the car, call Alex. Once he knows about Cody, he'll protect him. Whatever you do, don't go back to your place, that's the first place he'll look."

Shelby glanced at the note in her hand, her frozen mind trying to untangle Trina's request. She'd assumed, from Trina's frantic call, that her sister and husband had had another fight. But this sounded much more ominous. "I don't understand. Who will look for us? And who's Alex?"

For a long moment Trina stared at her, and then motioned to Cody, still buried deep in her arms. "Alex was my contact. He's also Cody's real father. Let's go. We don't have much time."

Stunned, Shelby gaped at her sister. What? Her contact? Cody's real father? What about Trina's husband, Stephan Kirkland? She cast her memory back in time. Trina had married Stephan a few months after Cody had been born. Of course, she, like everyone else had assumed Cody was Stephan's son.

"Does Stephan know?" Shelby bit back the urge to ask about Cody's biological father, conscious of little ears.

Trina nodded, but kept looking around the deserted marina as if expecting someone to show up. "Stephan isn't listed as Cody's father on his birth certificate. And he can't help. But Alex can. Keep Cody safe, Shelby. Promise me you'll keep him safe."

"Safe from what? Did something happen? Why would you have a 'contact'? Are you some sort of undercover agent?" Zillions more questions whirled in her mind.

Trina waved an impatient hand. "No, I'm not an agent. And none of this matters right now. We have to hurry. Cody's in danger. All I need from you is to keep my son safe. Will you do that for me? Please?"

It wasn't like her sister to beg. "Of course." Shelby loved Cody more than anyone on this earth. He attended Shelby's Little Lambs Day Care Center for preschool and stayed overnight at Shelby's more often than not. The thought of Cody being in danger made her feel sick to her stomach. She couldn't bear it. Was her sister over-reacting? Trina tended toward the dramatic. "I'll keep him safe, but I'm sure we can work this out together. We can go to the police for help."

Trina shook her head. "No. You have to leave now. Don't trust anyone, especially the police. Promise me you'll call Alex. That number is a secure line and you need to use that phone. Tell him it's been *twelve nights* since I've seen him last, that way he'll know I sent you. Don't call *anyone* but Alex. Understand?"

"No, I don't understand. Why can't *you* call Alex? Why can't we all go together?" Stubbornly, she stayed where she was, refusing to budge even though Trina's tension was palpable.

"I am coming with you. But if we get separated… don't come after me. Grab Cody and run. Let's go, we need to hurry."

Giving in to her sister's urgent fear, Shelby quickly shoved the phone and scrap of paper into her jacket pocket, and hoisted Cody up into her arms. Deeply thankful that Trina was coming with them, she turned to head back toward the brightly illuminated parking lot. Trina fell into step alongside Shelby, her gaze still intently sweeping the area.

"Please tell me what's going on," Shelby begged. "Why are you and Cody in danger?"

"It's safer for you if I don't explain," Trina whispered. "I've made a terrible mistake, but Alex will know what to do. He knows what's going on."

She wanted to ask more, but decided to wait until they were safely on their way. They were over halfway to her car when Trina sucked in a sharp breath.

"What?" Shelby shifted Cody's weight in her arms, trying to look past his bulky coat to see whatever had caused Trina's sound of distress.

"Run, Shelby! Don't stop for anything. Do you hear? Don't stop no matter what happens." Trina paused momentarily to brush a hand over her son's head, then veered to the right and sprinted in the opposite direction from the parking lot, heading back toward the wooden walkways leading to the rest of the boats suspended in their raised slips for the winter.

"No! Wait! Don't go. Come with us—" Too late. Shelby's eyes widened in horror, her feet glued to the dock as she saw a figure dart into view from behind one of the outbuildings heading straight for Trina. The figure lifted his arm and a sharp retort split the air.

A gun! He was shooting at Trina!

Instinct pulled at her to help her sister, but she remembered what Trina had told her. Shelby clutched Cody tight and surged into high gear, running for the safety of her car as fast as she could with the added burden of Cody's weight in her arms.

Cody began to cry. She whispered words of comfort between panting breaths. They were near the parking lot. She wanted to glance back to see what happened to Trina, but didn't dare. Had the gunman followed Trina? Or was he right now coming up behind them? She strained to listen, but could only hear the whistling wind.

Braced for the pain of a bullet, she bit back a sob and shifted Cody to the side, groping for her keys. Jamming her thumb on the key fob, she unlocked the door and scooted Cody into the passenger seat. She slid behind the wheel, twisting the key in the ignition. She yanked the gearshift into Drive, while she craned her neck around, to search for her sister.

Along the shore, two figures continued to run. The smaller one stayed several yards in front of the larger one. Shelby gasped, when the larger figure pointed his weapon at Trina. Another gunshot ripped through the air.

The smaller figure went down. And didn't move.

"No!" Sobbing, Shelby gunned the engine and swerved out of the marina parking lot, nicking the edge of a nearby light pole. Fear that the gunman would now turn his attention toward her and Cody fueled her panicked desire to get away. She fumbled in her coat pocket for the phone Trina had given her. She dialed 9–1–1, telling the operator that someone was badly hurt down at the lakeshore.

When the dispatcher pressed for more information, she sobbed, "Just go!"

Her careful wording hadn't fooled the little boy beside her. Tears streamed down his face. "Aunt Shelby, is Mama hurt?"

She swiped the dampness from her own eyes and struggled with what to tell him. He was only four-and-a-half years old. He should be home asleep instead of running for his life from a man with a gun. Her heart hammered in her chest. She took a deep breath to steady herself. She needed every ounce of courage she possessed. His safety depended on her.

"Yes. But the police are on their way to help her." She prayed it wasn't already too late.

Dear Lord, protect Trina. Please keep her safe.

Solemn green eyes regarded her steadily, breaking her heart. "Did the bad man get her?"

The bad man? A chill slithered down her spine and she clenched the steering wheel to keep her hands from shaking. She wished, more than anything, that Trina had told her exactly what was going on. "Did you see the bad man, Cody?" Could this be why his life was in danger?

He nodded, silent tears streaking down his cheeks.

No! Was this Trina's mistake? Allowing the bad man to see Cody? Her stomach clenched with fear. She pulled her nephew close within the circle of her arm. He buried his face in her side and she held him tight.

"It's okay, Cody. I love you. Everything is going to be just fine. We're safe. God will protect us." She kept her foot hard on the accelerator, speeding through the early morning darkness, taking various turns and changing direction often, in case the gunman had friends who might come after her. At this hour, the streets were empty. After she was certain no one had followed and that she and Cody were safe, she headed toward the main highway.

Don't go to your apartment, that's the first place he'll look. Call Alex. Don't trust anyone, even the police. Only Alex. Understand?

Careful not to jostle Cody, she pulled the slip of paper from her pocket, and divided her attention between the road and the scribbled note. The handwriting wasn't Trina's, but a deep, bold stroke of a pen, with the name Alex McCade and a local phone number.

She had no idea who Alex McCade was—other than Cody's father—but Trina seemed to think he would keep them safe. Trina had sacrificed herself to help them escape, so she had no choice but to trust Trina's judgment. With renewed hope, she glanced at her nephew, nestled against her side.

"Don't worry, Cody. Everything is going to be fine. We're going to find a man who can help us."

Alex McCade prowled the length of his room, rhythmically squeezing a palm-sized foam ball in his right hand. The throbbing pain in his arm often kept him up at night, until he thought he might scream in sheer frustration, but he wouldn't give up his efforts to rebuild the damaged muscles. The bottle of narcotics sat unopened on his nightstand. No matter how intense the agony in his arm, he refused to take them.

After a few minutes of pacing, the wave of pain receded to a tolerable ache. With a sigh, he paused before the sliding glass doors to stare outside where dawn peeked over the horizon.

Deep in the north woods of Wisconsin, there were no city lights to distract the eye from the wonder of nature. A blanket of fresh snow from the most recent March snowstorm covered the ground and coated the trees, illuminating the area around his sister's rustic bed-and-breakfast with a peaceful glow. A perfect, secluded area to recover in.

His sister, Kayla, had welcomed him with open arms. Things were quiet here, she didn't do as much business during the long winter months.

The muscles in his right forearm seized up, the intense

agony making him gasp. The foam ball fell from his numb fingers and he clutched above his wrist with his left hand, massaging the injured muscles into relaxing again. Every time he exercised his damaged arm, the same thing happened. The muscles would spasm painfully, forcing him to abandon his exercise regimen.

Helplessly, Alex stared down at the numerous surgical scars that crisscrossed his right arm from wrist to elbow. He didn't want to admit the plastic surgeon who'd spent long hours reconstructing his damaged muscles and tendons might be right. That his gun hand might never return to one-hundred percent. He should be grateful that he hadn't lost the arm completely, yet it was difficult to remain appreciative when his career, his reason for living, teetered on the brink of collapse.

The muscles in his arm loosened and he breathed a sigh of relief. Bending down, he picked up the foam ball and this time, kept it in his left hand. To strengthen the muscles, he opened and closed his fingers, squeezing tight. If he couldn't use his right arm, he'd build up his left. Anything to get him off medical leave and back on duty.

He needed to finish the case that continued to haunt him. For personal reasons of his own, he'd dedicated his life to being a DEA agent. For this case, they'd joined forces with the coast guard, in an effort to identify the mastermind behind the drug trafficking from Canada through the Great Lakes down to Chicago. Working undercover, he knew he was close the cracking the case before he'd been jumped by two men with knives. During his attempt to get away, they'd slashed his arm to ribbons and it had been too late to replace him. His coast guard partner, Rafe DeSilva, was doing his best to pick up the thread of the investigation.

Five years of work might be lost forever if he couldn't get back in the field soon.

He desperately needed to bring the brain behind the drug smuggling operation to justice. To do that, he needed to train the muscles in his left hand to become his dominant one. He didn't want to sacrifice his career for nothing.

His private secure cell phone rang. Startled, he dropped his foam ball in his haste to reach for the phone. Gritting his teeth, he forced himself to use his left hand as he warily answered. "Hello?"

"Is this Alex McCade?"

The female voice didn't sound quite right, considering the number indicated the call was from Trina Kirkland, his contact within the Jacobson Marina and shipping business. "Who's this? Who gave you this phone?"

"Trina gave it to me. I'm supposed to tell you it's been twelve nights since she saw Alex last. She also said Alex would help us—me." There was a brief pause and he heard the woman's voice break as if she were struggling to hold back tears. "Please tell me you're Alex McCade."

"Yes, this is Alex." Whoever this woman was, she knew the code phrase he had always used with Trina. What had happened? What had gone wrong?

"I need your help. It's a matter of life and death."

Life and death? His gut tightened with anticipation. Followed by a wave of guilt. He was currently on medical leave. If she was legit, he'd need this woman to talk to Rafe. He shoved the helplessness aside. "I'm going to put you in touch with Rafe, he's with the coast guard."

"No!" Her voice rose to a hysterical pitch. "Trina told me to call you. Only you. No one else. There was a man with a gun. I need your help, please!"

Alex blew out his breath, sensing the woman was tee-tering on the edge and one wrong word would send her tumbling over. His gut also told him she wasn't involved in the criminal activity surrounding the shipyard. He couldn't deny the possibility of a setup, but too much caution could be dangerous. Trina must have given her phone and the code phrase to this woman because her life was in jeopardy. The panic in this woman's tone was too good to be faked.

"What's your name?" he asked.

There was a brief hesitation. "Shelby."

"Where are you right now?"

"Near a town called Shawano."

Shawano was almost two hours away. Perfect. He'd have plenty of time to arrange a backup plan in case this woman wasn't who she claimed to be. "Okay, I'll give you directions to a truck stop in another town. From there, call me again to get further instructions."

He rattled off the directions, satisfied when she repeated them back correctly.

"So you'll meet us—me at the truck stop?" she asked.

"Not exactly." He knew if he mentioned his plan to have Rafe check her out first, she'd get upset again. Rafe would be discreet. She'd never know he was there. "I need to make sure you're not followed."

"Oh. Okay."

"Trust me, we'll be in touch soon." He hung up and immediately called Rafe.

"Yeah?" His partner sounded half-awake.

"I need backup. Can you be here in an hour?"

"What's up?" Rafe sleepy voice disappeared.

"Something has happened to Trina."

"Trina?"

Rafe's voice had sharpened and Alex knew his partner was finally awake. "Give me a few minutes and I'll call you back."

Alex picked up his foam ball and squeezed rhythmically with his left hand as he waited for Rafe to return his call. What had happened to Trina? He hoped she was all right. He couldn't help feeling that he should have been there with her. He hated being on the outside of the case, instead of working it from center stage. It was already mid-March and the ships would hit the water the first of April. He only had two weeks to get his left arm in shape to be his dominant hand.

For now, once he'd determined the woman, Shelby, was legit, he'd have no choice but to turn her over to Rafe.

Driving on the highway toward the truck stop with a clear destination in mind helped Shelby keep her rioting emotions under control. She could do this, one step at a time.

While Cody slept, Shelby battled grief as her thoughts dwelled on Trina. She knew, with gut wrenching certainty, that her vibrant, live-life-on-the-edge sister was dead. When they were younger, opposite personalities kept them from being close. Shelby was Christian and had never embraced her sister's free-wheeling lifestyle, but in the past five years Cody had managed to bring them together.

Shelby was grateful for that time when they'd been

closer, but the truth was she hadn't really known Trina, and now she never would.

Their father would be devastated by the loss. He thought the sun rose and set in Trina. He'd always ignored her mistakes, the bad choices that had time and again landed her in trouble. Shelby sniffed loudly and blinked back tears. Trina had gotten in trouble again, but this time she'd made the right choice. Trina had sacrificed her life for her son.

How would the little boy deal with losing his mother on top of meeting a father he didn't know? Now that she knew Stephan wasn't his father, she understood why Cody had spent more time with her than Trina and Stephan over the past few years. It was no secret her sister and her husband were having marital problems. Stephan and Cody had never been particularly close. Now Cody's whole life had been turned upside down.

And he was in danger. She could only hope and pray he didn't realize how much.

Cody stirred, waking up after his short nap. Sleep had been the best thing for him after all the trauma of the morning's escape from the marina. Pushing her steep exhaustion aside, Shelby smiled at him reassuringly. "Hey, are you hungry?"

He rubbed his eyes with his fists and nodded.

There was another small town coming up and she'd noticed a sign for a fast food place. "We'll pick up some breakfast in the next town, all right?"

After making a quick bathroom stop inside, they placed their order in the drive-through lane. Shelby fastened Cody back into his toddler seat, and watched him munch on his breakfast sandwich through the rearview mirror. She wasn't sure how much of Trina's conversation about him being in danger he'd picked up on, so she tried to distract him. "Guess what? We're heading into the north woods."

Cody's eyes widened, his interest piqued as she'd hoped. "Are we gonna see bears?"

"Nah, they're hibernating for the winter. But we might see deer." She took a sip of her coffee, hoping the caffeine would jump start her system now that the adrenaline rush had worn off.

"What about wolves? Or coyotes?"

Shelby shook her head, grinning wryly at Cody's fascination with wild animals. "I don't know, maybe."

Cody loudly slurped his chocolate milk through a straw. Steady green eyes regarded her in the mirror. "Aunt Shelby?"

"Hmm?"

"Am I gonna live with you now, forever?"

Shelby sucked in a harsh breath and tightened her grip on the steering wheel. *Yes,* she wanted to shout. *Yes, you'll stay with me forever.* But the words clogged her throat. Did Cody sense the truth about his mother's death? Did he know he was in danger? What was the best way to have this conversation?

Lord, give me some guidance here. How should I tell him? Please, Lord, help me find the best way to explain this.

"I don't know, Cody. Maybe." She took a deep breath and let it out slowly. "First we're going to visit your other dad."

"My other dad?" Confusion wrinkled his brow.

"Yes. You're a very special boy, Cody, because you

have two dads. The dad you've been living with and your other dad."

"After the visit, then I'm gonna live with you?" he persisted.

She wanted him to. Very much. Not right after the visit, as Cody had said, since they were still in danger. But once all of this was over… Still, she had no way of knowing if Alex, his biological father, would have other plans. Stephan wasn't listed as Cody's father and he'd married Trina after Cody's birth, which meant Alex would have the edge, if he wanted custody. The idea made her stomach hitch. She didn't know anything about Alex. Would he be a good father? Maybe she should find a way to disappear, keeping Cody with her forever.

As much as she wanted to do just that, her conscience wouldn't let her. The thought of the bad man knowing Cody saw him scared her to death. Would the man know Cody was with her? Was that why Trina had told her not to go back to her apartment over the day care center? She couldn't take a chance. No matter what the future held, Cody's safety had to be her first concern.

And regardless of who Alex was, he had a right to know about his son.

"I don't know, Cody. I hope so. We'll see."

Instantly his face crumpled. "I don't wanna go back to the marina! I don't like it there. I wanna stay with you."

"Shh. Hey now." Shelby reached her arm back around the seat to rub his leg. Trina and Stephan had lived near the marina. It didn't make sense that he was so afraid of going back there. "Cody, don't cry. I love you. I'll stay with you no matter what. I promise." She wished she could pull him into her arms, inhaling the sweet scent of his baby shampoo. But they needed to get to the truck stop as soon as possible. "I love you," she repeated. "I'll stay with you always. Okay?"

Cody swiped at his eyes and nodded, stifling his tears.

It was a rash promise but she didn't care. Because even if Alex claimed custody of his son, she wasn't leaving Cody. Alex would just have to deal with her being an important part of Cody's life, whether he liked it or not. She was not letting this boy go without a fight.

At the truck stop, she called Alex again on Trina's phone.

"I'm sure I wasn't followed," she told him. "No cars stayed behind me and I passed the exit, before doubling back."

"I'm sure you weren't followed, either."

She frowned, wondering how he could be so certain, but listened intently as he gave her specific instructions on how to get to the bed-and-breakfast where he was staying.

"I'll see you soon." Shelby snapped Trina's phone shut.

The sun was high in the sky when she turned onto Oakdale Road. Covered with freshly fallen snow, there were no recent signs of a snowplow. She hoped her lightweight, fuel-efficient car wouldn't get stuck.

She pulled into the bed-and-breakfast driveway, winding through the trees until she saw the house. She gaped in surprise at a huge log home lined with numerous windows. A massive deck encircled the house giving rooms on the second floor access to the outside. The grandness of the place intimidated her. This was a bed-and-breakfast in the north woods? She'd expected something smaller. Quaint. Cozy.

With a sigh, Shelby hefted Cody into her arms

since he was without snow boots. Her jeans were quickly covered in snow up to her knees as she trudged up to the house.

A tall, rugged, dark-haired man answered her knock and seemed surprised to see her standing there with a child. His piercing green eyes weren't at all welcoming.

"Alex McCade?" She shifted Cody's weight on her hip.

"Yes." A deep frown furrowed his brow.

"I'm Shelby."

He hesitated, his eyes darting to the boy before he opened the door wider. "Come in."

A welcoming scent of pine surrounded her as she stepped into a warm great room with a huge stone fireplace lining one wall. Through an arched doorway to the right, Shelby saw several tables draped with bright red and white checkered tablecloths. For a bed-and-breakfast, the place was notably vacant.

She stomped her feet on the braided rug, trying to dislodge as much snow as possible. Cody wiggled impatiently in her arms, so she set him on his feet beside her. Now that she was face-to-face with Alex McCade, she couldn't seem to find the right words to tell him about his son. Especially since his tall, broad presence was more than a little intimidating. She cleared her throat. "My name is Shelby," she said again. "And this is Cody."

Cody suddenly clutched her leg, hiding his face against her jeans as he wailed. "No! I don't wanna visit my other dad!"

She winced and tried to untangle Cody from her leg, casting Alex an apologetic glance. "I'm sorry, I didn't mean for you to find out like this."

For a heart-stopping moment, the man stared at

Cody. Then his cold, furious gaze cut to hers. "Is this some sort of sick joke?"

Swallowing hard, she thrust her jaw defiantly. "No, this isn't a joke. Cody is your son and I need your help to keep him safe."

TWO

His son? Alex stared at the woman, seconds stretching into a full minute. His heart froze in his chest. His stunned gaze fell to the child clutching the woman as if his life depended on her. The woman moved gracefully as she bent toward the crying child, quietly beautiful in a whole-some way, he noted as he continued to stare in shock.

Rational thought quickly soothed his initial panic. Her claim couldn't possibly be true. Tall and reed thin, with long curly blond hair and bright blue eyes, she looked familiar. But not to the point where he could have possibly fathered a child with her.

"You're lying." He glared at her, as if willing her to tell the truth. "Was this why you called? To make these ridiculous accusations? I thought you needed help?"

"We do need your help. Cody's in danger. But I wouldn't lie. Not about this. I'm sorry, I know this must be a terrible shock to you." The troubled expression in her eyes bothered him, as if she really cared what he thought and how he felt. "You have to believe Cody is your son."

He didn't have to believe anything. Alex's steely control over his anger slipped. "Look, I don't know what game you're playing, but I'm not amused."

"No game." The woman sighed and placed a protective arm around the boy. "Let me start at the beginning. My name is Shelby Jacobson and this is Cody. We live in Green Bay and…"

"Wait a minute." The pieces to this jumbled puzzle were finally sliding into place. He should have realized it sooner. Shelby Jacobson was Trina's sister. He knew Trina and Stephan had a son but he didn't know Shelby had a child, too. Not that he'd paid much attention to Trina's younger sister, since Shelby wasn't involved in the marina or the shipping business. She ran some sort of Christian day care center. "You're Trina's sister. That's why she gave you her phone to call me, right? Did she tell you she was in trouble?"

Shelby nodded, looking relieved. "Yes. But we're all in trouble, now. Trina promised you'd keep us safe. And she said you'd tell me what's going on. Trina mentioned you're her contact. What is she involved in? What's going on at the marina? Exactly what is the source of the danger?"

He curled the fingers of his injured hand experimentally. The pain was better now. He wasn't completely useless but he'd probably need to call Rafe if they were in danger. "I'll answer your questions the best I can but right now, you might know more than I do."

She opened her mouth to say something, but he quickly interrupted. "Don't worry, you're safe here," he assured her gruffly. "I'd never turn away a woman and her child, no matter who the father is."

Her gaze narrowed with annoyance, but he pivoted and gestured toward the great room. His eyes fell once more on the boy, who stopped crying long enough to stare at him with wide green eyes, identical to his own. A sick feeling settled in his gut. Irritably, he thrust it away. "Come in and take off your coats."

"Thank you," Shelby murmured helping Cody remove his bulky jacket before shrugging out of hers. She tossed them over a nearby chair and then crossed over to the wide sofa facing the tall fireplace.

Alex sent Rafe, his coast guard liaison, a quick text message telling him that he'd be in touch soon. Rafe was on standby, after having checked out Shelby at the truck stop to make sure she hadn't been followed, but Alex wouldn't require backup yet. He needed time to figure out what happened to Trina that forced her to give her sister the code phrase and her phone.

The boy climbed up next to Shelby on the couch and pressed against her. She put a protective arm around his shoulders. The two shared the same golden shade of blond hair and the same stubborn chin.

His sister Kayla came into the great room, sending him a wary glance before greeting Shelby. "Hi, I'm Kayla. I don't want to interrupt, but I just finished making a batch of chocolate chip cookies." She flashed Cody a warm smile. "Are you interested in sampling a few?"

Cody eagerly looked up, then hesitated and shook his head, scooting closer to Shelby. Alex frowned. What was the boy so afraid of? He tried to wipe the scowl from his features. "Kayla's cookies are the best. And you'd better get a couple, before Clyde finds them."

Cody threw him a puzzled look. "Clyde?"

"Our new cocker spaniel puppy, although no matter how many times we tell him that he's a puppy, he still thinks he's a boy, spending his entire day trying to eat people food." Alex wrinkled his face in mock disgust as he sat in a nearby chair.

The lure of a puppy who liked people food was too much to resist. Cody's gaze shifted between Alex and Shelby, his tiny brow furrowed as if leaving Shelby's side was a monumental decision.

"It's okay, Cody. I promise I won't leave without you. Go ahead and see the puppy." She let him off the hook, seemingly relieved at having him out of the way. Alex understood she was scared and wanted answers. But what exactly did Shelby have to gain by claiming the boy was his son?

She'd claimed they were in danger, but he needed to know exactly what happened, what had brought them here. After all, Trina had been his inside contact, not Shelby.

"Okay," Cody agreed readily enough but moved reluctantly away from her.

Kayla held out her hand. Cody trustingly took it. "You know, I have a daughter about your age. Her name is Brianna and she's spending the day with her grandmother. Maybe if you're still here later this afternoon, you'll get to meet her." Kayla chatted to the boy as she led him into the kitchen.

Shelby turned toward him with a look of abject horror etched on her face. "You have a *daughter* about the same age as Cody?"

Alex hissed a long breath between his teeth. "Kayla is my sister, not my wife. And let me make one thing perfectly clear. You and I did not create a child together."

Her eyes widened in frank dismay. "Of course we didn't. Cody is Trina's son."

For a moment he was taken aback. Then he scowled. "You mean he's Trina and Stephan's son."

"Trina told me you were his biological father." Shelby twisted her hands in her lap although he admired how she kept her voice steady. "Cody was born September tenth, roughly four years and six months ago. And Trina gave me this." She reached into her pocket and pulled out a crumpled slip of paper.

Alex took the scrap of paper from her and stared at his own handwriting in shock. This was the initial note he'd given Trina all those years ago, after their night together.

"She told me that once you knew about Cody being your son, you'd help keep him safe."

Unable to sit still, Alex jumped up to pace the length of the room. How was this possible?

One night. They were only together for one night. He swallowed hard. "Okay, but if that's true, why wouldn't Trina have told me that she was pregnant? Why marry Stephan?"

"I don't know. Trina didn't confide in me, either."

He jammed his fingers through his hair in frustration. Alex met Trina shortly after arriving in Green Bay. He'd been trying to dig up information on a tip about possible drug trafficking in the area. Trina seemed to know all about the boats entering and leaving the harbor so he had asked her out a few times to see if she'd let anything slip.

He hadn't meant for things to go so far. He wasn't proud of his actions, and had distanced himself from her after the night they'd spent together.

"I knew Trina had a child, but when Trina married Stephan a few months after the boy was born, I assumed the child was his," he admitted in a low tone.

"Frankly, I was relieved that she'd moved on to someone else after our night together." And he'd never made the mistake of getting too close to anyone on the job ever again. "So why have you decided to spring this news on me now?"

"Because Cody's in danger. And Trina obviously thought you needed to know he was your son, in order to protect him. Early this morning, Trina called and asked me to meet her down at the marina. She asked me to take Cody and made me promise to call you. She was going to come with us, but then…" her voice trailed off.

A chill snaked down his spine and he stopped in the center of the room, slowly turning to face her. On the phone she'd mentioned something about a man with a gun. "And then what? What happened?"

Shelby hesitated, worrying her lower lip between her teeth. He glanced at her upset expression, feeling an uncharacteristic spurt of sympathy for her, before abruptly turning away. *Don't go there,* he warned himself. He'd help Cody and Shelby but becoming emotionally involved was out of the question.

"On the way to my car, Trina spotted someone. She told me to run and she took off, heading back toward the marina. I caught a glimpse of a man with a gun. I—I grabbed Cody and ran."

"And Trina?" Alex forced himself to ask, although he could guess what happened next by the stricken look in Shelby's gaze.

"I think he killed her." Shelby's voice was barely above a whisper. "I dialed 9–1–1 but…"

Alex winced, unable to bear the frank pain in her eyes, crossing over to where Shelby sat on the edge of the sofa. He couldn't imagine how terrified she must have felt—witnessing an attack on her sister.

"She risked her life to save us," Shelby continued, her eyes welling with tears. "She drew the gunman away, sacrificing herself to safe her son. Your son."

Awkwardly, he sat beside her and placed his injured arm around her shoulders. For a moment she held herself stiff, but then sank against him, burying her face in his chest. Muffled sobs reached his ears and his shirt became damp with tears, but still he held her close. He murmured soothingly even as his hand delved into the softness of her hair. The sweet, spicy scent of it teased his nostrils. Holding her soothed him, too. Trina's death was a shock. She'd put her life on the line for them, to help bring the drug smugglers to justice. Who had killed her?

"I'm sorry." Shelby sniffled loudly and pulled away from his embrace. "It's just that every time I think of trying to tell Cody that his mother might never come home, I get all choked up. How do you tell a four-year-old something like that?"

Stunned, the full implication of her statement hit him like a snow-laden log falling on his head. If Trina was dead, and if he was the boy's father, then he was the child's only living parent. Ten minutes ago he hadn't known he had a son, much less one he might be solely responsible for. "Wait a minute, maybe there's some mistake...."

"I don't think so." Shelby misunderstood his murmured comment and took a deep shuddering breath. "I saw the guy aim at her and shoot. She fell to the ground and didn't get up."

Alex fought back a surge of panic. A father? No. This couldn't be happening. He wasn't father material.

Look at the role model he'd had. His old man drank too much and hadn't hesitated to lash out if he and Kayla said the wrong thing. Alex had vowed he'd never have children.

Yet, Cody had his green eyes.

Taking a deep breath he concentrated on identifying one problem at a time. It had been dark and Shelby only thought she saw her sister get shot. Even if she fell to the ground, Trina may have survived. Trina knew how to take care of herself.

He focused his attention on the problem at hand. Shelby and Cody needed protection from whomever had attacked Trina. Trina had been leaking information to the coast guard and DEA for the past two years, playing a very dangerous role. Someone on the drug smuggler's payroll must have caught onto her. She may have gotten careless, digging too hard to find proof that Alex was targeting the wrong suspect. Whatever she'd found, he could only imagine she'd been shot to keep her mouth shut. He couldn't help but wonder what she'd learned, and if her theory had been right. She'd vowed her father was innocent, but Alex had never been totally convinced.

Drugs were coming in on Russ Jacobson's ships and Alex believed that Jacobson had to know what was going on right under his nose. In Alex's opinion, Jacobson himself could be the mastermind behind the entire drug smuggling operation.

But did that mean Russ Jacobson was capable of having his own daughter killed? It was a stretch, but without proof one way or the other, he had no way of knowing for sure.

"Tell me what's going on," Shelby pleaded.

"It's complicated," he warned. "But first, are you sure the person with the gun was a man? Did you see him clearly?"

"No, I couldn't see him much at all, but I'm pretty sure he was a man." Shelby stared at him, her brow furrowed. "And in the car when we were driving away, Cody asked me if the *bad man* hurt his mom."

"What? You mean *Cody* actually saw the guy?" This news changed everything. The danger was worse than he'd imagined if Cody was a witness to the potential leader behind the smuggling.

Alex eased away, trying to unobtrusively disentangle his hand from her hair. The silky strands seemingly had a will of their own as they clung to his fingers. He glanced toward the kitchen where the boy had disappeared. "I need to talk to him."

"Oh, no you don't." Shelby's tone was sharp and she tugged on his arm when he moved to get up. He hid a wince as a tender nerve zinged with a shaft of pain. "Not until you tell me what's going on. Besides, Cody has been through an awful ordeal. He practically saw his mother being murdered. I don't want him to relive the horror all over again so soon."

"But if he's seen the bad guy, maybe we can get a description or at least something to go on." Alex understood her reluctance to expose the boy to more distress, but this was a possible murder investigation. Not to mention, a potential lead to the organizer behind the drug smuggling ring. Trina's murder was obviously linked to his case. Or rather, to Rafe's case.

"Maybe you can talk to him later," she hedged. She stood up and walked closer to the fireplace, as if needing the warmth. "I brought him here so that you'd keep him safe. We need to protect him, not traumatize him."

Alex frowned, understanding her logic to a certain extent. But decided to let the subject go for now when Kayla and Cody emerged from the kitchen trailed by the clumsy puppy.

"Shelby, look at Clyde," Cody said happily. "Isn't he great?"

"He sure is." Shelby's face softened into a warm smile and Alex couldn't dismiss her obvious love for the boy.

In a daze, Alex did the mental math and came to the conclusion that the timing was right for him to have fathered Cody, although for all he knew Trina could have been sleeping with both him and Stephan at the same time. He'd request a DNA test at the very least, so that he would know for sure.

During the time he'd been undercover as a long-shoreman, he hadn't seen Trina's son at all. Wisely, she'd kept him far away from the unsavory characters who had often hung out at the docks.

One look at Cody now, though, told him almost as much as a DNA test. At first he was so focused on Cody's blond hair, he hadn't really looked at the rest of his facial features. He could see that aside from the hair and the stubborn chin, Cody was the mirror image of himself at that age. Kayla had a box full of their baby pictures in the attic to prove it. The kid's green eyes haunted him.

Not the kid, he admonished himself. *My son. I'd better get used to the fact that Cody could really be my son.*

Shelby knelt beside Cody and scratched the pup behind the ears. "So how were the cookies? Did Clyde get any?"

Cody giggled as he petted the puppy. "No. Dogs can't eat people food. It's bad for them, 'specially chocolate. The cookies were good, but not as good as yours," he loyally added.

"I can show you to your rooms." Kayla's intensely curious gaze bounced back and forth between the three of them. "That way you'll have some time to freshen up or to take a nap, if you prefer, before dinner."

"Oh, well—" Shelby's hesitant gaze swung around to collide with Alex's.

Alex raised a brow at her dismay. Clearly Shelby hadn't thought any further than tracking him down. Logically, he knew he should turn both of them over to Rafe. But now that they were here, he'd rather keep them close at hand. At least, until he'd gotten a chance to talk to Cody.

"Kay's right. You're both safe here, so there's no point in you leaving to go somewhere else. Especially when this place has more than enough room." He flashed a crooked smile, waving a hand at the various rooms overhead. "There's plenty of privacy, I'm the only guest at the moment."

Shelby drew in a long breath, reaching up to rub at her temple. "All right, then," she agreed slowly. She stabbed him with a fierce glance. "But we still need to talk."

Alex hesitated, glancing down at Cody who was watching them both curiously. "We will, but for now, why don't you get settled into your rooms. I have some phone calls to make."

"Me, too," she said with a frown.

"That's not a good idea. You can't tell anyone you're here or what you've seen," he warned. "I'll explain more later."

He could tell she wasn't happy with being put off, but she also clearly didn't want to say much in front of Cody. Obviously she took her role of being the boy's protector very seriously.

Slowly she nodded. "All right." She turned to Cody. "Should we check out our rooms, partner?"

The boy nodded, although his attention was focused on Clyde who jumped up on him, trying to lick him in the face. Within moments the two were rolling on the floor with Cody giggling madly over the puppy's enthusiastic affection.

Alex felt his chest tighten at the sight. He glanced up to find Shelby staring at him intently. For a long moment, they exchanged a look full of understanding. Hers reinforced that she would protect Cody at all costs. His admitted the need to take things slow, so he didn't scare the boy.

He watched them walk up the stairs, grappling with the knowledge that he could deny the truth all he wanted, but he was likely Cody's father.

What he was going to do about it, he had no clue.

Shelby's earlier fear slowly began to fade as she gazed at her surroundings, while Kayla gave them the nickel tour. They mounted the staircase to the second story. The log home was even more impressive inside. A cathedral ceiling towered overhead giving an expansive view over the great room from the loft encircling the second floor. When Kayla showed them two adjoining rooms, Shelby saw that her earlier assumption was correct. Each room contained patio doors leading out onto the snow-covered deck.

"The shared bathroom is through this door here." Kayla crossed the room to demonstrate. "And you can leave the connecting door open, if you prefer."

"You have a beautiful home." Shelby admired how the furnishings in the room had a rustic look, from the overstuffed chairs to the pine, sleigh-shaped bed frame. For the first time since leaving the marina in a mad rush, fully expecting the gunman to come after them, she felt safe. Secure. Because of Alex?

Kayla's mouth formed a sad smile. "Thank you. My husband had a hand in building it himself, before he died."

"I'm sorry." Shelby inwardly winced at her blunder. She couldn't imagine how difficult it would be for a woman to raise a child alone after her husband's death.

"That's all right." Kayla straightened, shaking off the despondency. "He died nearly two years ago, but he was a wonderful man. And I'm not totally alone, his mother helps me by watching over Brianna when I'm busy working. Well, here I am jabbering in your ear, when all you want to do is relax for a bit. Dinner will be ready about six. If you're hungry before that, just come down to the kitchen. There's always plenty to eat."

"Thank you." When Kayla left, Shelby closed the door behind her and glanced over at Cody. He didn't usually take naps, but his eyelids drooped as a result of his interrupted night. She wasn't feeling too perky herself and the white down comforter on the bed looked soft and inviting. "So, partner, how about we lie down for a few minutes?"

"I don't wanna lie down." A wide yawn belied his words but he pried his eyes open, fighting fatigue the way kids tended to do. "Are we gonna live here now? I like Clyde."

Shelby shook her head, eyeing the puppy that had followed them upstairs, claiming Cody as his newfound friend. Clearly, every child should have a pet. She made a mental vow to get Cody a dog of his own once this mess was over. Would Alex mind? No, she wasn't going there. If she wanted Cody to have a puppy, he'd have one.

"We can't live here, Cody. In the spring and summer, these rooms are rented out to guests. We're just lucky there isn't anyone here now." Inspiration struck. "Would you like to take a nap with Clyde?"

"Yeah!" Cody ran into his room, the puppy close on his heels. Her ruse worked, forestalling further questions about his father or their possible future together. She wouldn't be able to dodge the little boy's questions forever.

But first and foremost, Cody needed to be safe. Once they were out of danger, she intended to ask Alex to grant her sole custody. The apprehensive expression in his eyes, when he'd looked at Cody, convinced her that he wasn't overly thrilled to be a father. Which was fine with her. She couldn't have loved Cody any more if he really were her son.

Cody would feel better, once he knew what to expect in the future.

Shelby left open the adjoining door between their rooms, so that she'd hear Cody when he awoke. She slid between the sheets, sighing gratefully as the down mattress cushioned her tired and aching body. Sleep should have come easily.

Instead Alex's face swam in her mind, interrupting her search for blessed oblivion. She couldn't believe she'd cried on his shoulder. She hadn't leaned on a man in a long time, and Alex wasn't exactly the best candidate. He was too intimidating by far. And besides, maybe he wasn't married, but he'd clearly been irresponsible all those years ago.

Instantly she felt ashamed. She couldn't pass judgment on him for having an intimate relationship with Trina, since she wouldn't have Cody in her life if he hadn't.

But she didn't get the sense he held the same Christian beliefs she did. She'd found God as her savior after an awful experience in college, where she'd narrowly escaped being sexually assaulted. She'd found solace in God and her church, and the people there had helped her again after she'd suffered a brutal attack at the shipyard a few years ago. She'd overcome her fear of men slowly but surely, with help from the Lord. Creating her Little Lamb's Day Care Center had helped her find a greater purpose in life. She hadn't planned to have children of her own—she wasn't sure she'd ever trust a man enough to risk her heart—but she'd love to raise Cody as her son.

Shelby knew she was getting ahead of herself, since she didn't really know what Alex's plans were, so she tried not to dwell on him. Or his relationship with her sister. She trusted him only as far as his ability to keep them safe.

Nothing more.

Tossing and turning in the unusually soft bed, her unanswered questions swirled through her mind. What had Trina been involved with? What was the source of the danger? Who had Cody seen?

She couldn't help a tiny flash of guilt. Maybe she should let Alex question him, get some answers. But she knew all too well what it felt like to be a victim. She didn't want to cause Cody to have nightmares like she'd had. The poor kid needed time to assimilate what had happened.

And really, how much detail would a four-year-old be able to give in a description, anyway?

She wondered what was going on back in Green Bay. She didn't talk often to her father, but surely he'd find out soon about what happened to Trina. She'd have to call him. And what about Stephan? Had Stephan discovered the truth about Cody's biological father last night? Was that the reason Cody was in danger?

No. She couldn't believe Stephan was the *bad man* that Cody had mentioned. Up until now, Cody had called Stephan *dad* even if they were never really close.

Too many questions and she grew irritated with Alex for not giving her nearly enough answers.

She must have fallen asleep because she abruptly woke up, blinking groggily in the darkness, instantly aware of her strange surroundings, wondering what had woken her so suddenly. In a rush she remembered the bed-and-breakfast, and Alex. Outside, dusk had fallen, telling her she had slept longer than she'd planned. Quickly pulling on her clothes, she poked her head through the connecting doorway, her gaze searching for Cody.

His bed was rumpled, but empty.

She paused to listen for sounds of him playing with the puppy downstairs, but everything was quiet—though not for long.

The sharp retort of a gunshot from somewhere outside ripped through the silence of the night.

"No!" Shelby ran downstairs, barely pausing to grab her coat from the chair before she threw open the door. Her mind raced with terrifying thoughts of what she might find as she barreled out into the frigid moonlit night desperate to find her nephew.

THREE

Shelby peered through the night, forcing her eyes to adjust to the darkness. The snowy ground showed a trail of footprints. She thrust her arms into her coat sleeves even as she slipped and stumbled on the icy trail of trampled snow leading back around the house. The darkness swallowed her. Concern for Cody overpowered her usual fear of the night.

"Cody!" Shelby began to shout as she dodged between trees. Her voice sounded distant through the roaring in her ears. She noted another building—a pole barn, hidden in the woods to the left of the house. A shaft of light shone through the small side door left ajar. "Cody?"

Another gunshot ripped through the air, louder this time. With a sob of horror, Shelby burst through the door. She glanced around wildly. Alex stood in the center of the room holding a gun, wearing a pair of earmuffs.

Alex pulled them off the moment he saw her.

"Shelby? What's wrong?" In an instant, he crossed over to her, lightly grasping her arm.

Helplessly, she shook her head, choking back tears and gasping for breath. Her heart pounded frantically in her chest. "I—I woke up and Cody wasn't in the room. And th-then I heard gunshots."

Chagrined, he glanced over to the target he'd clearly been using. "I'm sorry. I should have realized you'd worry."

"The last time I heard gunfire, my sister was shot." She couldn't help pinning him with an accusatory look. A burst of anger quickly replaced her gut-wrenching fear. She tore from his grip, curled her fingers into a fist and smacked him square in the chest. "What on earth possessed you to shoot off a gun?"

He frowned and glanced down at the weapon in his hand, as if noticing it for the first time. "I needed to work on my arm. It's not what it should be. Considering you came here for protection, I thought I'd better practice. I'm sorry. I wasn't thinking about Trina."

She stared at the long paper targets hanging over sheets of plywood propped in front of several bales of hay stacked in the back of the shed, forcing herself to think logically. Alex wasn't the bad guy here. He was Trina's contact which meant he must be a good guy. And he was Cody's father. He was just trying to protect them.

Shelby drew a deep, shuddering breath. For years, she'd avoided men, but suddenly now here she was, totally dependent on Alex for safety. The idea was extremely disconcerting.

She let go of her anger, knowing her overreaction wasn't his fault. Since his goal was to protect them, how could she argue?

She glanced at Alex, and he shook his head at the unspoken questions in her eyes. "Let's go back to the house," he suggested. "So you can see for yourself that Cody's fine."

Shelby slowly nodded, following him outside down the path she'd taken a few minutes ago.

When a low hanging branch tangled in her hair, she tried to yank free, muttering under her breath.

"Here, let me help." Alex came up behind her and deftly unhooked the naturally curly lock of hair from the branch. His nearness made her shiver and not necessarily with fear. She stepped away. She shouldn't be tempted to lean on Alex, not when she'd fought so hard to remain independent.

"Thanks." Her breath shortened and she hunched her shoulders, careful to duck far below the trees. His calm presence managed to distract her from her fear of the dark.

Alex must be a cop. That would explain why Trina sent them to him for protection. Her preoccupation with her sister caused her to stumble over a fallen branch, half-hidden beneath the snow. Alex caught her by the arm.

"Watch your step." Alex frowned when she instinctively pulled away from his touch. He glanced down at her sodden feet. "We need to get you a pair of boots. Kayla's already loaned Cody a pair of Brianna's."

"We left Green Bay in a hurry." Shelby grit her teeth together to stop them from chattering. Alex's domineering personality put her on the defensive. She wasn't used to anyone questioning her parenting skills. "Besides, we didn't have as much snow there as you do here."

"I'm sure Kayla has a pair that'll fit." Alex kept his hand under her elbow as they climbed up the few steps to the house.

Shelby refrained from answering. Safe inside the

well-lit house, she breathed a sigh of relief. She'd conquered the darkness, at least for a few minutes. Feeling foolish for her rush of panic, she removed her coat and her sodden tennis shoes. Her jeans and socks were damp, but she ignored the discomfort, simply walking toward the sound of voices coming from the kitchen had died down in their absence.

When they entered, Cody ran up to her. She caught him close in a quick hug, which he tolerated for a half a second before squirming away. She reluctantly released him.

"Aunt Shelby, were you practicing shooting with my other dad outside? When I get older, he said he's gonna teach me how to shoot a real BB gun."

"Oh, really?" Calmer now, Shelby sent Alex a narrow look. Just who did he think he was making a promise like that, without even asking her? No matter what biology said, he was *not* Cody's only parent, and he had no right to make decisions like that without consulting her. She didn't approve of guns and she especially didn't approve of teaching children how to shoot them. Shelby held on to her temper with an effort, turning her attention to Cody. "Who's your new friend?" she asked, gesturing to the girl standing near the stove with Kayla.

"That's Brianna. She's five. Clyde's her puppy, but he likes me better."

Shelby rolled her eyes at the rivalry in his tone. "I'm sure Clyde likes you both the same. Are you hungry, or did you eat dinner without me?"

"No, of course not," Kayla said. "Brianna, you and Cody need to set the table."

"Okay," Brianna agreed as she dashed toward the

cabinets on the other side of the kitchen, dragging Cody with her.

"I'm sorry," Kayla murmured, her gaze apologetic. "I didn't realize you'd heard the gunshots until I saw you running for the door. I wanted to come after you, but I couldn't go outside like this." She pointed down to her feet, covered only in thick socks.

Shelby tried to smile. Cody was safe and that was the important thing. "It's okay. I'm just not keen on guns."

"Guns are only a problem when they're misused." Alex spoke testily. "Don't worry, I keep trigger locks on all my weapons."

All his weapons? How many did he have? Shelby wasn't about to stand around, debating the pros and cons of gun legislation with him. Not on the same day when she'd watched someone shoot her sister. In fact, she was glad Cody was doing all right in here, and hadn't reacted to the noise of the gunshot with the heart-wrenching fear she'd felt. Maybe he hadn't seen as much during their frantic dash to the parking lot as she'd thought. Gathering every ounce of patience, she steered the conversation toward a safe topic. "So, what's for dinner?"

"Venison stew," Kayla replied.

"Venison?" Shelby tried to hide her dismay.

Kayla chuckled. "That was my reaction too, at first. But trust me, you'll like it."

"Don't tell me it tastes like chicken."

Kayla laughed. "Why don't you two go have a seat in the great room?" she suggested. "I'll call you when everything's ready."

Back in the great room, Shelby noticed that the fire had died down. She reached for a log, intent on adding to the dying embers, but a masculine arm snatched it from her grasp.

"Here, let me. You need to change into some dry clothes."

Annoyed, Shelby wondered if all men liked to pretend they were in charge of the world, or if this was a characteristic unique to Alex McCade. She might be afraid of the shadows, but years of living alone had taught her to fend for herself in her own way. She valued her independence and preferred to keep it that way. Dire circumstances had brought her here. She needed Alex to keep Cody safe. She did *not* need him to boss her around.

She sat on the edge of the sofa, propping her feet on the stone hearth of the fireplace. "I don't have anything else with me. Besides, I'm fine."

"I'm sure Kayla will lend you a few things."

"I'm fine," she repeated stubbornly. She didn't want to put her hostess out any more than she already had.

"I know you're upset with me," Alex murmured in a low tone. "I promise I'll try to answer your questions. But I don't want to talk in front of the kids." Alex waved in the general direction of the kitchen, where Cody and Brianna were still helping Kayla by setting the table.

Shelby lifted her gaze to his. He wasn't looking at her, though, but stared thoughtfully into the fire. When he wasn't ordering her around, he was very attractive, not that she had any business noticing. He wasn't at all her type, even if she wasn't interested in men, which she wasn't. Considering her past experiences, she didn't trust men on a personal level and that included Alex. "They won't hear us if we're quiet. Be honest with me. Are you in law enforcement?"

"Sort of." He shrugged and glanced at her. "I work for the government."

Her eyes widened. "FBI?"

He shook his head. "DEA. Shelby, you'll need to keep everything I tell you confidential. Your life and Cody's depends upon it."

She swallowed hard at the seriousness of his tone. "Okay."

Alex took a deep breath and let it out slowly. "How much do you know about your father's shipping business and the marina?"

"Not a lot. Most of my time is spent running my day care center." Shelby wrinkled her forehead, realizing she'd have to call her assistant soon to let Debbi know she wouldn't be there on Monday. "Trina and Stephan manage the marina."

"I know. Trina was helping us, providing inside information."

Shelby frowned. "Like what?"

"Details that may be pertinent to us finding the drugs being smuggled into the U.S. from Canada through the Great Lakes. Names of ships, routes, etcetera. We're trying to find the identity of the mastermind behind the drug smuggling operation. We knew there were several insiders, including one in customs, but we needed to find the guy in charge."

"Drugs? On my father's ships?" She stared at him in shock. "You can't be serious."

"Shelby, I saw the shipments firsthand. I was working undercover as a longshoreman, reporting to Bobby Drake, the warehouse foreman and your father's right-hand man. During the time I spent on the docks, I discovered drugs coming in on your father's ships over and over again. That much is fact. What we don't know is who's responsible."

She sucked in a harsh breath. She'd had no idea. "You think my father is involved, don't you?"

"I saw him on the docks a fair amount. He kept his hand in every aspect of his business. Russ Jacobson was especially interested in the cargo on the ships that traveled from Sault Saint Marie to Green Bay, with the final destination being Chicago. The same ships where we found drugs."

"No!" Shelby jumped to her feet, her hands fisted at her sides. "I'm telling you, Alex, my father isn't involved in drug smuggling."

"Shh." He frowned at her, and then glanced over his shoulder toward the kitchen where the kids were playing with Clyde. "Calm down. Trina felt the same way you do. Yet we have no choice but to treat everyone as a suspect, until proven otherwise. You wanted to know the source of the danger, well this is it. Whoever hurt Trina must have figured out she was feeding us information."

"Dinner's on," Kayla called.

Alex glanced toward the kitchen. "We'll discuss this more later."

Shelby didn't want to discuss it later. She wanted to talk about it now, so she could show Alex he was wrong. Yet in spite of her instinctive defense, she felt uneasy. She wasn't an idiot. Her father's shipping company dominated the Great Lakes shipping business. How could drugs be on his ships without his knowledge? She shoved aside the shimmer of doubt. She didn't know how her father had missed what was going on, but she was relieved to hear Trina believed in their father's innocence, too.

She was tempted to insist he tell her more, but bit her tongue, in deference to Cody. The poor child had been traumatized enough. He didn't need to hear his aunt arguing with his *other dad.*

"Yes. We will talk more later." Her gaze warned him that she expected answers. He returned her look with a bland one of his own.

Kayla called out to them from the kitchen. "Are you coming?"

They both hurried into the kitchen. Instead of eating in the formal dining room usually reserved for guests, they crowded around the oak picnic table in the kitchen. There should have been plenty of room, especially when Cody insisted on sitting next to Brianna. Yet Alex seemed to take up more than his share of space. His presence was disturbing and not just because she usually avoided being so close to a man. For some strange reason, his woodsy aftershave teased her senses.

"Excuse me," she muttered when their elbows bumped for the third time. She scooched over a few more inches. Any farther, she'd be sitting on the floor.

"Switch places with me, I'm left-handed." Alex lifted his plate and stood while she slid into his spot so that he could sit at the end.

He was still too close. His right hand rested on the table and Shelby could see a few of the reddened scars above the denim cuff of his shirt. What had happened to him? Mesmerized by the dark sprinkling of hair on his forearm, she didn't realize she'd eaten half her stew until Kayla snickered at her from across the table. Flustered, she stared at her bowl. Had the meat tasted different? She couldn't say one way or the other.

"What do you think?" Kayla asked.

She flashed her a sheepish smile. "You're absolutely right, Kayla. The venison stew is wonderful."

"Thanks. Alex is a hunter and he shot the deer himself, last year." Her voice rang with pride.

"Can I learn how to hunt deer?" Cody piped up from the other side of the table.

"No."

"Sure."

Both Shelby and Alex answered simultaneously. She threw him a dark look. Alex had the grace to look away guiltily.

"I don't think you'll be old enough to hunt for quite a while yet, Cody," Shelby amended, noticing the confusion in the boy's eyes. She mentally cursed Alex for interfering. She'd been making decisions regarding Cody's upbringing for years, how could he expect to suddenly step in and take over?

Because he's Cody's father. Shelby's appetite vanished and she stared down at her half-eaten food. The thought of losing Cody to Alex twisted her stomach into a hard knot. She loved Cody. She couldn't love him more if she'd borne him herself. What if Alex took him someplace far away where she'd never see him again?

Her fork clattered to her plate from fingers gone numb.

"Shelby? Are you okay?" Alex sent her a glance so full of concern she nearly blurted out the truth. Only a deep sense of self-preservation made her hold her tongue.

"Sorry. I'm just clumsy I guess." Shelby tried to smile, but her face felt as if it might split in two with the effort.

Drugs coming in on her father's ships. Cody's bad

man. Trina's death. Suddenly it was all too much. Obviously she needed Alex, in order to keep Cody safe, but a tiny part of her just wanted to grab Cody and run away from it all. But that was the problem, wasn't it? All alone with Cody would she ever be able to stop running? She couldn't condemn Cody to that kind of life. He was safer here with Alex. For now.

How she made it through the rest of dinner, she'd never know. Afterward she excused herself from helping with the dishes and retreated to her room long enough to use Trina's phone to place a call to their father and then to Debbi, her assistant manager of the day care center. Shelby didn't intend to break her promise to Alex, but needed to at least find out about Trina. Maybe her sister had miraculously survived.

Punching the numbers on the phone pad, she dialed her father's number. A woman's voice drifted over the line after the third ring.

"Hello?"

Shelby swallowed her annoyance when her father's wife answered the phone. She didn't particularly care for the woman who'd become their stepmother. "Hi, Marilyn. Is Dad around?"

"Shelby? Your father's worried sick. He's been trying to call you for hours. What is wrong with you? You should be here with him. Don't you care about him at all? Where are you?"

Shelby winced at her shrill voice. "Please, Marilyn, stop yelling at me. Just put Dad on, would you?"

"Fine. Be that way."

Marilyn dropped the phone with a clatter making

Shelby pull the instrument away from her ear. After a few minutes, her father's booming voice came over the line.

"Shelby? Where have you been? I've been calling your place all day."

"Sorry, Dad." Shelby tried not to back down from his accusatory tone, but it wasn't easy. Her relationship with her father wasn't great. When her mother was still alive, they'd been a close-knit family. Every Sunday, after church, they'd have family game night. She'd cherished those times. But things had gotten worse after her mother died. Her father had changed. Ever since her mother's death he'd been trying to toughen her up, trying to make her into something she wasn't. Someone like Trina. Most of the time she avoided her family, preferring her friends from church to the rowdy crowd who hung around at the marina. Her father never hesitated to vocalize his disapproval.

"I've been worried about you. Do you have Cody?"

"Yes, Cody's with me. We're safe. Everything is fine," she hastened to reassure him.

"So you haven't seen Trina, then?"

She hesitated, not wanting to lie, but not wanting to break her promise to Alex, either. "Not in a while," she hedged. To the best of her knowledge, no one had known that she was meeting Trina down by the marina. Cody had often stayed with her when her sister was working.

"Then you don't know." He let out a heavy sigh. "There's been a terrible accident, Shel." For a moment, he sounded like the father she used to know. The one who taught his young daughters how to sail on the waters of Lake Michigan. "Your sister..." He struggled to get the words out. "Someone shot her. She's dead."

Shelby closed her eyes against a wave of grief, even though she'd suspected the worst all along. To hear her father state the truth so bluntly was harder than she'd anticipated. "What—what happened?"

"I don't know." The helplessness in his tone was so uncharacteristic that Shelby wished she were with him. "I can't think of anyone who'd want to kill her. Of course I called the mayor, asking him to make Trina's murder a priority. It pays to have friends in high places. So far, Lieutenant Holden thinks it's a robbery, since all of the jewelry Trina had been wearing was stolen, including her wedding ring."

Her father sounded lost and forlorn, reinforcing what Shelby had known all along. He couldn't possibly be involved in something so heinous as drug smuggling, and he certainly played no part in Trina's death. A part of her wanted to blurt out the truth, how she'd seen the dark figure shoot Trina, but she held her tongue. For Cody's sake. "I'm sorry, Dad."

"Where are you? You said you have Cody with you? Because Stephan has been wondering where he is."

"I have Cody and we're staying with a friend." She frowned. "I know Stephan and Trina were having problems, and that Trina had moved out, but I'm sure this is still very hard on him."

"Yes. I was hoping they'd work things out." He sighed heavily. "Why don't you come home? I need you, Shelby. Trina—the police haven't released her body yet, so we haven't scheduled the funeral."

The funeral? A fresh wave of tears threatened and Shelby blinked them back with an effort and rubbed the scar at her temple.

Of course she and Cody would be expected to attend the funeral. But would that be good for Cody? Was it safe enough for him to attend? She honestly didn't know. "I'm sorry, but I can't come home right now, Dad. Please don't worry, we're fine. And I promise I'll stay in touch."

"See that you do." Russell Jacobson's tone hardened. "I know your church views prevented you and your sister from becoming close, but our family needs to stick together in times like this."

His words were sharp, an arrow piercing her heart. Her father had taken this attitude, acting as if her Christian path was somehow the wrong one, maybe because she'd found so much comfort in her church community, rather than with her family. "We weren't that close, but I loved Trina. And I love you, too. I'll call you later, Dad."

She snapped the phone shut before he could say anything more. A battery of emotions assailed her: grief, fear, anger, despair, loneliness. And of course, above all, guilt. Her father had a knack for making her feel guilty, even for events beyond her control.

Brushing away the evidence of her tears, Shelby stood, took a deep breath and squared her shoulders. Trina trusted her to keep Cody safe and that was exactly what she'd do. From here on out nothing mattered except the small boy who hadn't deserved to be dragged into harm's way.

Shelby crossed the room to the patio doors that led to the snow-covered deck surrounding the house. Troubled by her conversation with her father and her concerns about Cody's future, she gazed into the darkness outside. She didn't dare go home, not if that meant Cody would be in danger. But she knew her father was worried. With a sigh, she rested her forehead against the cool glass.

Dear Lord, guide me. Show me the way.

Shelby needed to seek God's guidance. Because no matter what she wanted, she had to do whatever was best for Cody.

Feeling calmer, she lifted her head and took several deep breaths. For a moment, she basked in the wonder of God's beauty, the snow-covered trees surrounding Kayla's log home and the occasional star twinkling in the velvet sky.

A bobbing light captured her gaze. She sucked in a quick breath and swiped at the fog on the glass. Intensely, she peered at the wooded area to the left side of the house.

The light was gone. She blinked, wondering if she'd imagined it. Maybe the events of the past twenty-four hours had gotten to her.

Shelby stood, indecisively. Maybe her tired mind had played tricks on her, but what if someone really was out there? She couldn't ignore the slim possibility.

She needed to find Alex.

FOUR

"Alex!" Shelby's serious tone made him spin away from the fireplace in the great room to look up at where she stood, leaning over the rail in the loft. "I think someone could be outside."

"You saw someone?" Immediately his senses went on alert.

"I saw a light. But it was gone so fast, it might have been my imagination." Shelby ran down the steps to meet him in front of the fireplace, her blue eyes round with alarm. "Is it even possible that Trina's shooter found us? Where's Cody?"

"Playing video games with Brianna." He wasn't surprised her first concern was for the boy. He couldn't bear the thought of either Shelby or Cody being in danger. He pushed aside his fear for their safety to think logically. A light in the woods? Could be a poacher with a flashlight. Or possibly Rafe? He'd asked Rafe to stake out the truck stop to make sure Shelby hadn't been followed. Had Rafe come out to the B & B to provide backup? Maybe. Maybe not. He'd need to investigate, to confirm. "I'm not sure how the shooter could have followed you here. It's probably nothing. Stay here. I'll check things out."

She caught his arm, preventing him from leaving. "Alone? Maybe I should go with you."

Did she think he couldn't handle himself? He frowned. He'd protest her with his life, if necessary. "You stay here, with Kayla and the kids. I'll be fine."

With excruciating slowness, her slim fingers loosened their grip on his arm and dropped away. The bare skin of his forearm tingled from her touch. Maybe his injured arm was overly sensitive from the damaged nerves.

Ignoring the strange sensation, he grabbed his coat and shoved his feet into sturdy snow boots. He grimaced, realizing he'd left his handgun in the shed after Shelby had gotten so upset.

He went into the cold night. The darkness was absolute. Black clouds obliterated most of the stars that might have illuminated the sky. He stood on the porch for a moment, his back against the wall of the log cabin, while he scanned the area.

Nothing seemed off-kilter. He dug his cell phone out of his pocket and texted Rafe.

R U outside the B & B
No in town

He stared at Rafe's response and debated whether he should explain about Shelby seeing a light or not. Shelby was tense, skittish. Could be she only thought she saw a light. Or more likely, saw a flash of headlights from the highway.

Need backup?

Rafe texted again.

No stay put.

Icy snow crunched beneath his boots as he made his way down the porch steps and around the side of the house. He didn't turn his flashlight on right away, preferring not to announce his presence if someone was out there. He took his time, stopping frequently to listen and look.

No telltale signs of lights anywhere.

Moving quietly, he made his way around to the left side of the house, along the path they'd taken earlier from the shed. He edged along the aluminum side of the shed. His gun was inside, but he didn't want to alert anyone by going in. He peered around the corner. For long seconds, he didn't move.

Nothing.

No owls hooting as they hunted for prey.

No white-tailed deer making their way through the trees searching for food.

No wolves roaming the night.

The lack of wildlife, or at least the sounds of wildlife, nagged at him. Sometimes animals could sense a pending storm. The thick clouds overhead reinforced that theory.

But sometimes they also sensed the presence of an intruder.

He slipped through the woods, finally turning on the flashlight and making a broad sweep around the house until his wounded arm ached with cold. There was no evidence of strange footprints in the undisturbed snow.

Shelby must have seen headlights through the trees, nothing more. He made another sweep around the house, and then convinced there was no immediate threat, he headed back inside.

Shelby glanced up at him expectantly from the corner of the sofa, one of Kayla's colorful quilts wrapped around her.

"Didn't see a sign that anyone has been here other than us," he said, as he toed off the snow boots. He crossed to warm his right arm by the fire.

"I know what I saw," she protested, her voice low and husky.

"I believe you." And he did. But Shelby was a city girl and this was the forest. They were far away from the civilization she was accustomed to. "Could have been a poacher, or maybe lights from the highway. We know you weren't followed here, so try not to worry. I'll keep you and Cody safe. No one will get past me to harm you." He couldn't hide the husky note of protectiveness in his voice. "I'll bunk here on the sofa tonight, just to be sure."

She captured her lower lip between her teeth, but didn't say anything as her faintly questioning gaze clung to his.

Mesmerized, he couldn't look away. Shelby was beautiful, in a softer, more unpretentious way than her sister. She was hesitant and shy where Trina had been bold and vivacious. Yet every minute he spent with Shelby, he found himself drawn to her. There was something about her that made him feel possessive. Protective. Alive.

And when she gazed at Cody, the love shining from her eyes made him ache with longing.

The crackle and pop of the logs in the fireplace only added to the charged atmosphere. He swallowed hard, inhaling the warm scent of cinnamon and spice that seemed to cling to her.

Focus, McCade. Concentrate on the case.

He cleared his throat. "Don't worry. I can get backup here quick, if we need it."

She frowned a little. "Backup? Like other DEA agents?"

"No. Like Rafe, my liaison with the coast guard. The DEA teamed up with the coast guard in order to break the drug smuggling ring." He glanced at her, hoping she wouldn't get upset about using Rafe for help, the way she had on the phone, but she didn't.

"How long have you worked for the government?" Shelby asked.

His entire adult life. He'd joined the DEA to help fight the war against drugs. Because he'd lost his best friend in high school, Toby, to a horrible drug overdose. But she didn't need to know all that. "Long enough. In one way or another, I've been working on this case for well over five years."

"Over five years?" Realization dawned in her eyes and she sucked in a harsh breath. "Cody."

He winced at the reminder. He wasn't used to explaining himself, but for some reason, he was tempted to do just that. He didn't want Shelby thinking the worst of him.

"I swear to you, I didn't know he was my son."

She shrugged and tucked a strand of hair behind her ear. "I know. The look on your face…" She trailed off.

Then her expression closed up. "Your relationship with my sister is none of my business."

"We didn't have a relationship." His tone was blunt. "I—made a mistake. It was—well, we weren't in love or anything. I didn't see her again until several years later. After she agreed to help us." And by that time, their conversations had been short and terse, only about the case and nothing more.

She plucked at the threads on the quilt and then raised her guilty gaze to meet his. "Speaking of Trina, there's something you need to know. I called my father, using her phone."

"You what?" He ground his teeth together, trying to rein in his temper. "I told you not to tell anyone you were here, remember?"

"I didn't." She lifted her chin defiantly. In that moment, she reminded him of Trina. "I called my assistant at the day care center to let her know I wouldn't be in on Monday. And I called my father. But don't worry. I didn't tell anyone where we were or even who I was with. But my father confirmed Trina was shot to death at the marina." Her voice broke.

"I'm sorry," he murmured. He felt bad for Trina. Someone had figured out she was leaking information. But who?

"Thank you. The police are investigating," she went on. "My father is on friendly terms with the mayor and he's pressing for a quick arrest. Apparently Lieutenant Holden thinks Trina's death was the result of a simple robbery."

"Holden? Eric Holden?" he interrupted.

"I guess. Why?"

He knew Rafe had worked with Eric Holden, and

knowing Holden was involved in Trina's case made him feel better. As far as he could tell, Holden was a decent cop. In general, the Green Bay police department hadn't welcomed the interference of the coast guard and DEA. Eric had been the most accepting of the bunch, even if he hadn't fully bought into the theory of a Canadian drug running operation until they'd provided proof.

Would Holden give Rafe details about their investigation into Trina's death? Worth a try. He'd call Rafe first thing in the morning.

"Do you know him?" Shelby asked with a puzzled frown.

"I know about him from Rafe, but he doesn't know me. I worked deep under cover. And despite the standard line he gave your father, we both know Trina's death had nothing to do with a robbery. Trina must have stumbled into the truth behind this drug running operation. It's all linked to how the case started unraveling months ago." Three months ago, to be exact, when he'd been jumped and stabbed and set up to take the fall.

She reached up to massage her temple. "So now you know why my father couldn't possibly be involved in your case. Trina was his favorite. He loved her. If you could have heard him, you'd understand." She swallowed hard.

Alex didn't know what to say. A sense of unease washed over him. Trina had always claimed her father was innocent too, but he just couldn't be certain. It all seemed far too coincidental, how Russ Jacobson liked to be visible down at the shipyard. His interest in the ships coming from Sault Saint Marie to Green Bay and then to Chicago. The same ships where the drugs had been found.

Was he truly capable of killing his daughter, or ordering her death? The man behind the drug running scheme took innocent lives every day by exposing people, especially kids, to drugs. Not to mention, nearly killing him. He flexed his injured hand in surprise. Shelby's need for protection helped him to forget the pain.

Or maybe she just helped him understand there was more to life than just this case.

He shook his head at his foolish thoughts. For him there was only the case. Nothing more.

Shelby was right. The few interactions he'd witnessed between Russ and Trina indicated a deep fondness between father and daughter. But that didn't prove anything. When torn between love for his daughter and greed, who knew what he'd choose? And maybe there was someone else involved. Someone calling the shots, over Russ's head, or behind his back. There was a missing link, and he needed to find it to put this all together.

The sound of voices carried from the kitchen. Kayla's rooms were on the main level, tucked behind the kitchen and away from the guest rooms. Alex easily picked out Cody's excited tone rising above the din, asking if he could sleep with Clyde. Within moments, the boy laughed gleefully as he dashed through the great room, Brianna and puppy hot on his heels.

Cody saw him standing there and tried to stop but there must have been water on the floor so he slipped and skidded headfirst into Alex, cutting him off at the knees and nearly bowling him over.

As he regained his footing, Alex suddenly knew. The missing piece of the puzzle was his son.

"Sorry," Cody mumbled, when he disentangled himself from Alex and scrambled to his feet.

"No harm, no foul." Alex kept his tone light but inside, his emotions whirled. He desperately needed to question the boy, but the protective instincts vibrating from Shelby prevented him from pushing the issue. Besides, he couldn't help worrying about Cody, too. Could he afford to let his need to protect his son keep him from pursuing every lead on this case?

Cody wrinkled up his forehead. "What does that mean?"

Alex blinked, focusing on his son's curious face. "What? No harm, no foul? That just means I won't hold it against you, since you didn't hurt me."

"Oh." Cody still looked puzzled, and for the first time Alex wondered about the man who'd helped raise his son. What kind of father had Stephan Kirkland been to Cody? Did he spend Saturday afternoons pitching baseballs to the boy? Did they go hunting and fishing? Or to the movies together?

Did Cody miss him?

"Never mind." Shelby stood, shooting him an exasperated glance. "Cody, you need to go upstairs and get ready for bed."

"Okay. Brianna said I can sleep with Clyde tonight." The kid had a one-track mind and he'd focused it on the dog.

"How nice of her." Shelby flashed his niece a warm smile. Alex found himself wishing she'd smile like that for him.

"Brianna!" Kayla called from the other room. "You're supposed to be brushing your teeth."

The kids scampered in opposite directions and Alex turned to Shelby. "I have to talk to Cody. I need to know who he saw."

She stared at him for several seconds. "I know. But not yet." Fierce, she stood her ground. "I already told you, he's been through enough. Let him get a good night's sleep and then we'll see how he does."

"He's four years old. What if a good night's sleep makes it hard for him to remember what happened? Don't you realize he might be the key to cracking this case?" Alex raised his voice, unable to hide his frustration. He understood her protectiveness, he felt the same way, but honestly, how could a few questions hurt?

Shelby raised a hand to her forehead, grimacing as if she had a pounding headache. "Yes, I do. And I told you, we'll talk about it tomorrow. What more can you do tonight, anyway?"

He wasn't used to anyone questioning him, but at this point, he hated to admit she was right. Maybe it would be better for Cody to have a good night's sleep. "All right. Tomorrow then. No more stalling."

"I'm not stalling." Impatience laced her tone. "I want to know who is after him as much as you do. But I'm concerned about Cody's mental health, too. How much can a child take without breaking? What if all of this haunts him for the rest of his life?"

For a long moment, they stared at each other, on opposite sides of a line drawn in the sand.

Alex sighed in frustration. He strove to hang onto his temper. "I don't know," he allowed. "I don't want Cody hurt any more than you do. But I can't help if I don't know what the danger is."

"I thought you'd already had a list of suspects? Including my father." Shelby arched one brow. "If I recall correctly, you've accused Cody's *grandfather* of a despicable criminal act."

Stunned, he stared at her, unable to come up with a response to that. His son irrevocably tied his life to Russ Jacobson's. Lashing out at Shelby's father wouldn't win him any points. "I won't question Cody without your permission, okay? We need to work together on this."

Shelby eyed him warily for a tense moment. And then her shoulders slumped as if she'd been carrying the weight of a huge burden. "You're right. We need to work together."

He wanted to go to her, to ease the tension from her muscles. To pull her into his arms, offering comfort. Her features were fragile, as if another wrong word would make her break. She turned away, putting distance between them. "I'm going to put Cody to bed."

"May I join you?"

His question halted her midstep and she swung around to face him. "What?"

"I'd like to help put Cody to bed." Why was she staring at him like that? He tucked his hands into the pockets of his jeans. What did putting a kid to bed entail? Tucking him in? Reading a bedtime story? He hadn't done fatherly things with Brianna, and now he wished he had. He might be out of his league with this fatherhood stuff, but something made him stand there while Shelby stared at him in frank dismay. Maybe Cody didn't feel comfortable with him yet, so he'd act more like a father, starting now.

He couldn't protect Cody if his son didn't trust him.

"I—guess." Her stark frown of disapproval was not reassuring.

Alex almost let her off the hook, but held his tongue. With obvious reluctance, her back stiff and unyielding, she kept pace with him as they climbed the stairs together.

Inside his room adjacent to hers, the boy giggled as the puppy growled and pounced when his foot moved beneath the covers. The sound of Cody's childish laughter made Alex grin.

Shelby went over to Cody's bed and sat on the edge beside him. "Did you brush your teeth?"

Cody nodded vigorously. "Yep. Kayla gave me a toothbrush. How come dogs don't have to brush?"

"Because they have special treats that help keep their teeth clean." Shelby gently pushed the puppy aside, so she could pull the covers up to his chin.

"Why can't we use treats instead of toothpaste?" Cody persisted, more, Alex thought, to keep her talking than because he wanted to know. Either way, Alex noted Shelby never lost patience with Cody's stream of questions.

"Because people treats have sugar in them and sugar is bad for our teeth." She leaned over to hug and kiss him, even as he opened his mouth for another question. She forestalled it by placing a finger over his lips and giving him a no-nonsense look. "It's time for bedtime prayers."

As if someone flipped a switch, the boy quieted down. He pressed his tiny palms together and closed his eyes. "Dear God, please help me to be good and to follow Your path. Please bless Mommy and Daddy and Aunt Shelby and Clyde." There was a pause, and then he added, "And please bless my other dad, too. Amen."

"Amen," Shelby echoed softly.

Alex stared down at Cody, his throat was thick with emotion. Never in his life had anyone prayed for him.

He hadn't grown up going to church. Had he missed out on something important?

"Good night, Cody," Shelby was saying. "Remember, I'll be right next door if you need anything."

Alex darted a glance over his shoulder and saw that indeed, she'd left the door open between their adjoining rooms.

"Okay. Can I leave my light on?" Cody's gaze hesitantly darted to Alex as if worried he would refuse.

He stepped forward, seeking and finding the light switch in the bathroom. "How about if we leave the bathroom light on, but close the door a bit, like this?" He demonstrated what he meant.

Cody earnestly nodded his approval. "That's good."

Alex wondered if Cody had always been afraid of the dark or if this was something new. A surge of protectiveness enveloped him. For the first time, he understood Shelby's resistance. At that moment, he knew he wouldn't hesitate to stop anyone who threatened to harm his son.

"I love you, Cody," Shelby said, leaning over to finally give him a hug and a kiss. "Always and forever."

"Me, too." He hugged and kissed her back. Then looked up at Alex expectantly.

Awkwardly, he leaned down to smooth a hand over Cody's fair hair, in lieu of a kiss. "Good night, Cody."

"G-night." Cody pulled Clyde close within the crook of his arm. The puppy didn't seem to mind, lifting its head to lick the boy's cheek.

Shelby stood and together they left the room. She headed over to stand at the railing overlooking the great room. Alex sighed out his pent-up breath. He spoke without thinking. "That wasn't too hard."

She arched an eyebrow at him. "No, I suppose not."

He let out an exasperated sigh. "Why do I have the feeling you don't approve of me as Cody's father?"

Shelby flushed, but thrust out her chin stubbornly. "Because I don't. You have no clue what being a father really means."

Okay, she had him there. His role model was a work-aholic father who spent zero time with his kids. And when his dad wasn't working, he drank. He'd taken the brunt of his father's fits of anger to shield Kayla. Until he grew strong enough to defend himself.

But over these past few months, he'd bonded a bit with his niece, Brianna. So he knew a little about kids. Or at least, he'd learned to be comfortable around them.

Maybe he'd never been a full-time father, but Shelby's attitude bothered him. She'd known him for less than a day. Was she really willing to write him off so quickly? Alex hid his consternation under a cool look. "I'm a good uncle to Brianna, so it's not as foreign as you think. I'm sure Cody and I will figure it out together."

The color left her face as if he'd slapped her. Then he understood. Shelby was afraid he'd take custody of the boy, cutting her completely out of his life. What had she said? Something about Cody pretty much living with her for the past three years? Before he could hasten to reassure her, she spun on her heel and headed for her room, closing the door behind her with a sharp click.

He stared at the door, imagining she'd have built a barricade by hand, brick by brick to keep him far away from Cody.

And he didn't much care for the feeling of being left alone on the outside looking in.

* * *

Shelby washed her face, wishing she'd kept her mouth shut with Alex. She stared at her reflection in the mirror. What was wrong with her? Where was her Christian attitude now? God would not approve of her picking a fight with Alex McCade.

Alex was Cody's father. A tiny, selfish part of her knew she wasn't being fair to Alex because she didn't want to lose custody of Cody.

But Cody certainly deserved a father. Alex was a decent man who truly cared about his son. She needed to let go of her fears.

Before climbing into bed, she sank to her knees, bowing her head in prayer.

Forgive me, dear Lord. Help me to follow the path You have chosen for me, now and always. And please, Lord, give me the strength and the wisdom to put my trust in Alex. And to help him form his relationship with his son. Amen.

Feeling more at peace after opening her heart and her soul to the Lord, she crawled into the sleigh bed. Tomorrow would be a better day. She needed to work things out with Alex, no matter how difficult, for Cody's sake and for her own. She didn't want to be the person she'd been today—so anxious and frightened that she couldn't stop herself from lashing out.

No matter how tense and confused Alex made her feel on a personal level, she trusted him with her life. And Cody's.

A muffled noise woke her from a deep sleep. She blinked, straining to listen.

The sounds were coming from Cody's room.

She threw the covers aside and scrambled from her bed. Heart in her throat, she darted through the connecting doorway.

Cody sobbed, thrashing his head back and forth on the pillow. The puppy whimpered in tandem beside him. Her chest tightened and she pushed the covers away, gathering Cody into a warm embrace. His arms clutched her and he continued to murmur through the sobs.

"Shh. Cody, it's okay. I'm here." She rocked with him cradled against her chest. The puppy settled down, his tail thumping against the bed.

"Mama." He sobbed the word against her neck.

"I know, Cody. I know you loved your mama." She hesitated, and then gently told him, "Your mom is in heaven now, with God. She's looking out for you. I'm here with you, Cody. I love you very much. You're safe now." Shelby battled tears as she rubbed a hand over his back.

"Why did she talk to the bad man?" Cody asked, his plaintive voice muffled against her skin. "Why?"

Shelby froze. Was he aware of what he was saying? "You saw your mom talking to the bad man?" she asked, holding her breath, afraid of the answer.

He nodded, his sobs quieting. "Outside. At night. I saw them through the window."

Who had Trina talked to? And why? "Where was your dad?"

He shrugged. "I dunno. But I don't wanna have any more bad dreams."

"I know, sweetheart. I'm here with you now." She didn't have a psych degree, but she instinctively knew not to push him. The poor child had enough to deal with at the moment. "I love you, Cody. I will always love you."

"I love you, too." Chubby arms clung tightly around her neck and she shifted so that she could lean back against the headboard of his bed, keeping Cody nestled in her arms. Clyde edged closer, and pushed his nose under her hand, licking her fingers. She pulled the puppy into a three-way embrace.

She closed her eyes, reveling in the peace and quiet of the night. She didn't want to think right now. She just wanted to hold on to Cody and pretend that as long as she kept him close, he'd be safe. They'd both be safe.

FIVE

Shelby was half-asleep when she heard a soft knock.

"Cody? Are you all right?"

It took several seconds to pull herself together. "He's fine," she called out in a low, soft voice. "Just a bad dream."

Cody stirred a bit, but didn't awaken.

Alex opened the door and stepped farther into the room. His hair was tousled, as if he'd just gotten up. His concerned gaze fell on Cody. "I heard noises. Everything okay?"

"Fine," she whispered. She lifted a finger to her lips, indicating they should be quiet, but Cody stirred again and this time he groggily lifted his head.

"Is it morning?" he asked, his tiny brow puckered in a confused frown.

"No, it's still nighttime," Shelby reassured quietly. "Go back to sleep, Cody."

He yawned, and pried his eyes open. "What if the bad dream comes back?"

"Think of God and the angels up in heaven," she suggested. "I promise they're watching over you and they'll keep the bad dreams away."

When he didn't look convinced, she added, "I'll stay here until you fall asleep."

"And I'll be right downstairs, too, Cody," Alex added. "If you need anything, just holler."

"Okay." Cody snuggled down against the pillows, his little arm curling around Clyde. The puppy laid his head right next to Cody's.

Alex smiled and Shelby was surprised by the flash of tenderness in his gaze. Despite her earlier resentment, she was glad he was so concerned.

He backed out of the room, his gaze on hers and she waited a few minutes, until Cody's breathing relaxed, before she gently disentangled herself from the bed and followed Alex into the hallway.

She was amazed he'd heard them from downstairs. Had he heard her get up? And if so, just how much of their conversation had Alex overheard?

Alex stood, waiting for her in the hallway. She took a few minutes to compose herself, as she gently closed Cody's door behind her.

By silent agreement, they walked down the hall away from Cody's room, pausing outside the door to her room.

"Did he have a dream about the bad man?" he asked.

His question didn't surprise her. But still she hesitated, wondering how to respond. She knew he wanted a description of the man Cody saw, but what if Cody couldn't really give them one? The only new information she'd learned was that Cody had watched through the car window as his mother had talked to the bad man. And that bit didn't exactly provide clues he could use on the investigation.

"Yes, but he didn't remember much. Only that he

was afraid." Shelby tried to keep her gaze trained on Alex's face so he wouldn't sense the half truth. Right now, Cody needed his rest, and she was afraid to ask more questions while that night was fresh in Cody's mind. She tightly gripped the doorknob behind her, anxious to escape into the safety of her room. "I'm sorry he woke you."

In the dim light from the fire in the fireplace below, she saw him shrug. "I don't sleep well anyway, so it doesn't matter."

"Why not?" The question slipped out before she could check herself. She bit her lip, knowing his issues were none of her business. "Sorry, that was incredibly rude."

"That's okay." He lifted his arm and pulled up the sleeve of his soft denim shirt uncovering the angry looking surgical scars. "Pain tends to keep me awake."

Even in the dim light from downstairs, the scars looked horribly painful. She resisted the urge to touch them, wishing there was something she could do to help ease the hurt. "Isn't there something you can take?"

His lips thinned and he shook his head. "No."

A charged silence fell between them. Suddenly she realized he was close. Far too close. And it was dark. Old fears bubbled to the surface. She took a step backward and bumped up against the door. She felt trapped. Panic surged and she struggled to keep her breathing even, though it seemed something had sucked all the oxygen from the air around them.

"I have to get to bed. Good night, Alex." Twisting the knob in her hand, she opened her door.

"Wait." Alex clasped her hand and held fast, preventing her from leaving. "Don't leave."

The way his fingers clamped around her wrist sent a cascade of dark memories crashing into her mind. "Let me go," she hissed, yanking her hand from his grasp.

Instantly, he released her. She stumbled back against the door, trying to get as far away from him as possible, her chest tight with fear.

"I'm sorry." He stared at her, his brows pulled together in a dark frown.

As quickly as they caught her off guard, the horrible memories receded, followed by a wave of shame. What was wrong with her? This was Alex. He'd come up to protect them, not to hurt her.

"It's okay," she regained her footing and tried to sound normal even though her hands were shaking. "I'm fine. You just surprised me, that's all." She winced at the lame excuse and forced a smile. "I'll—uh—see you in the morning."

"Shelby…" he began, but then caught himself and stopped. He held her gaze and took a deliberate step back, giving her more room. "You're right. It's late. Get some sleep. We can talk in the morning."

"Sure." She gave a jerky nod, her heart still rapidly beating in her chest. "Good night."

"Good night, Shelby." His concerned gaze stayed on hers as she shut the door between them.

Mortified by her overreaction to Alex's touch, she crossed the room and knelt at the side of the bed. After closing her eyes, she took a deep breath and reached out in prayer.

Dear Lord, I know You sent me to Alex to keep Cody safe. I know You're watching over us. Please give me the strength I need to conquer my fears. Amen.

* * *

Alex silently trod down the stairs to the main level, pausing long enough to replenish the wood for the fire. For a long moment, he stared into the dancing flames, reliving that awful moment when Shelby had physically recoiled from his touch.

He felt sick knowing how badly he'd frightened her. He'd never physically hurt a woman in his life. Certainly he'd never threatened a woman on a personal level.

But there was no mistaking the stark fear in her eyes when he'd caught her arm in an attempt to prevent her from slipping away.

He sank onto the couch, using the heels of his hands to rub his eyes. Shelby hadn't seemed threatened by him earlier in the day. He shouldn't have grabbed her arm like that. He hadn't realized she'd think he would force her to stay with him.

His stomach churned. She was afraid of men. Deeply afraid, in a primal way he'd never imagined.

He knew she'd been attacked by a man several years ago, one night down at the shipyard warehouse. Did that night haunt her still? After all this time?

If so, it was his fault. Maybe if he'd acted quicker, he could have prevented Shelby from being hurt. At the time, as he'd watched the attack take place, he'd wanted to go after the guy who'd hurt her, but he couldn't afford to break his cover.

Bitter guilt surged and he shot to his feet, pacing the length of the room, trying to get a handle on his simmering emotions. He'd done the best he could.

But his best hadn't been nearly good enough.

Once he'd calmed down, he stretched out on the sofa, grabbing Kayla's quilt to ward off the chill.

Sleep didn't come easy. Somehow he knew he needed to gain Shelby's trust. He couldn't stand to think she'd ever be afraid of him.

He cared about her, more than he should. He wanted the right to keep her safe.

Even though he knew she could never really belong to him.

The next morning, Alex fought the effects of his sleepless night, stumbling to the kitchen before anyone else was up to make coffee. He would need gallons of it to get through the day.

He stared broodingly at the pot as it slowly dripped. When it was finished, he poured himself a mug and carefully carried it in his left hand back to the living room.

Using his left hand still didn't come naturally. He needed to return to the shed and do more left-handed target practice. His aim was getting better, though not quite good enough that he'd trust himself in the field. To protect Shelby and Cody, he'd need to be in top form.

And time was slipping away. Russ Jacobson's ships would be back in the water in less than two weeks. Which meant more drugs making their way into the hands of innocent kids. Whoever was responsible would be using this time to take care of all obstacles, roadblocks and witnesses, like Cody. He found the foam ball and began working the stiff muscles in his left hand.

When he heard Kayla moving about in the kitchen, he knew he should go in to help. But he wanted to see Shelby. To talk to her.

To reassure her that he'd never hurt her. He only wanted to protect her, and his son.

Soon he heard Cody's giggles and the clickity-click of Clyde's toenails on the hardwood floor. Seconds later, Clyde dashed down the stairs with Cody on his heels.

"The puppy needs to go outside," Alex warned.

"I know." Cody didn't seem to have suffered any ill effects from his nightmare as he let the dog out. The kitchen was empty, and he realized his sister must be with Brianna.

"You're taking really good care of Clyde," he said to Cody, trying to strike up a conversation so his son would feel more comfortable around him.

Cody's smile brightened his tiny face. "Can I feed him, too?"

"Sure. I'll have to help you with the bag of dog food, though." Alex lifted the thirty pound bag and carefully poured the contents into the dish Cody held. "See? We make a great team."

"Will I be as strong as you someday?" Cody asked, when Alex had set the bag down.

"Absolutely. I bet you'll even be stronger than me." He couldn't help wondering if Cody's desire to be strong had anything to do with what the boy had witnessed two nights ago with Trina. But he didn't ask. This wasn't the time or the place. Besides, he wanted Cody to be comfortable, not afraid.

"Where's your aunt Shelby?" He glanced up toward the loft.

"She's coming. I'm hungry."

He glanced around the kitchen. "Well, I could try

making breakfast," he started. But just then Kayla hurried out.

"I'll make breakfast. Cody, do you and Brianna want to help me make French toast?"

"Yeah!" Cody exclaimed, following Kayla and Brianna over to the cupboard where Kayla kept the powdered sugar.

Considering they'd only arrived yesterday, it was good to see the boy was already making himself at home. Kids were often more resilient than adults gave them credit for.

He heard Shelby coming down the stairs, so he went out to meet her. Her footsteps faltered on the stairs when she saw him. She smiled but her smile didn't quite reach her beautiful blue eyes.

Swallowing the lump of bitter regret in his throat, he tossed the foam ball onto the sofa and stood. He slid his hands into his front pockets to appear nonthreatening. "Good morning. Did you sleep all right?"

"Of course." The dark circles under her eyes belied her words and likely matched his own. "How about you?"

"Sure." If she could stretch the truth, so could he. "Ah, do you have a minute? I wanted to talk to you for a moment, about Cody."

"All right." Although she nodded, her eyes remained wary. She sat on the edge of the sofa, as if prepared to bolt.

He regretted their argument yesterday evening and wanted to find a way to reassure her about his intentions regarding Cody. He reached over and picked up a photograph off the end table. He handed it to her. "Here. Kayla found this in the attic."

Shelby's mouth dropped open as she looked at the small boy who was the mirror image of Cody, aside from the color of his hair. "Is this you?"

"Yeah. When I was about Cody's age."

"The resemblance is amazing." She raised her gaze to his. "Is this your way of telling me you believe you're Cody's father?"

Trust Shelby to get right to the point.

"Yes. I'm convinced." He took a seat across from her, still giving her plenty of space. "That's what I wanted to talk to you about. I don't know what the future holds for us, but I wanted to let you know, I do want Cody in my life, but I'll never keep Cody away from you. I've seen you interact with him and it's clear how much you love him. And he loves you, too. I would never take that away from either of you. You will always be an important part of his life."

"I—thank you."

For a moment his chest tightened when her eyes shimmered with tears.

"I'm the closest thing he has to a mother and he's been traumatized enough. Last night, he cried out for his mother during his nightmare. I tried to explain how she's up in heaven with God and the angels, but I don't know if he really understands."

He remembered Cody's prayers, but had thought that was just a childhood routine. "Do you really believe that?"

She looked shocked. "Of course. Don't you?"

He had vague recollections of going to church as a child, but that was long ago, before his father had started to drink. "I don't know. Maybe."

She appeared troubled by his response. "I plan to

continue to raise Cody as a Christian." It wasn't a question, and the way she angled her chin made it a gauntlet she'd thrown between them.

He wasn't sure what exactly that entailed, but he figured having Cody brought up with church beliefs couldn't hurt him. "That's fine."

Her shoulders relaxed a bit and he could tell she'd been prepared for an argument. "Cody's asking questions about where he's going to live. I know right now the focus needs to be on keeping him safe, but eventually we'll need to make some plans. He needs stability. Cody deserves to have answers, not more evasions."

"I know." He honestly wasn't trying to avoid the future, but there were more important things to worry about at the moment. "Does Stephan have any parental rights to Cody that I need to know about?"

"No. Trina didn't list him as Cody's father. And she had Cody before they were married. I'm certain he never formally adopted him."

The news should have been reassuring. But he couldn't completely get rid of a sense of panic. There was nothing standing in the way of him being Cody's father. What sort of father would he be? He wished he knew. "All right. We'll figure something out. Right now, the priority is to keep you both safe. I'm hoping to talk to Cody later today, if that's all right with you."

She hesitated and then nodded. "Yes. It's fine."

He glanced toward the kitchen where Kayla and the kids were having breakfast. "Let's get something to eat, shall we?"

In the kitchen, Kayla was in command, wearing a plain white apron tied around her waist as she manned the stove. The griddle sizzled as she cooked another batch of French toast. For a split second, Alex could easily picture Shelby standing there, making breakfast for him and Cody. The thought jarred him.

Where had that bizarre image sprung from?

He'd never looked for any type of permanent relationship before because in his experience, even those women who claimed they didn't want kids wanted more than he was willing to give. So why was he even thinking about it now? Especially with a woman like Shelby? A woman whose picture was likely in the dictionary as a definition of home and family.

She believed in God. Raising Cody as a Christian.

He didn't know the first thing about being a father. And he knew even less about how to raise a child to be religious. Who was he trying to kid? Being an uncle to Brianna wasn't the same as being a full-time father.

"Good morning," Kayla greeted them. "Grab a plate and help yourself."

"Thanks." Shelby poured a cup of coffee, and then turned to him, holding out the pot with a questioning gaze. He swallowed hard and nodded, holding out his empty cup for a refill.

Knocked off balance by the domesticity, he took a hasty sip and scalded his tongue. Served him right for imagining the impossible.

Forcing himself to use his left hand, he ate several slices of French toast, chuckling a bit when he noticed the powdered sugar smiles on Cody's and Brianna's faces.

"Kayla, I need to buy some clothes for us," Shelby said as she finished her meal. "Is there a place nearby you can recommend?"

Alex frowned, remembering that she mentioned yesterday how they didn't bring anything with them. "Do you have cash?"

She flushed with embarrassment and averted her gaze. "No, I'm afraid not."

"Shelby, I don't want you to use your credit or debit cards," he told her sternly. "Anyone with a little access could easily track you here."

She paled and glanced at his sister. "I didn't think of that. Kayla, would you be willing to loan me some money?"

Alex grit his teeth at the way she was avoiding him. Why was she acting like he was some sort of piranha? He pulled out his wallet and pulled out some cash, wishing he had more to give her as he tossed the money on the table in front of her. "Here. I have plenty. Let me know if you need more."

"That's too much," she protested, staring at the bills as if they might bite.

He slid a glance at Cody, who was earnestly talking to Brianna between mouthfuls of food. "Apparently, I have a few years of child support to make up for."

Her brows drew together in a hurt frown, and he wondered what he'd said to cause that reaction. Whatever the problem, she reluctantly picked up the money and stuffed it in the front pocket of her jeans.

"There's a large discount department store in town." Kayla piled her own plate full of food and sat down with them. "I'd offer to go, but I have a leak under the kitchen sink that needs to be fixed."

Alex raised a brow. "I'll take a look at the leaky pipe, Kay."

His sister's gaze dropped to his injured hand and he tensed when she shook her head.

"I've learned to do a lot of things since my husband died, including fixing minor plumbing problems. Maybe you should take Shelby and Cody to the store so they don't get lost."

"We'll be fine," Shelby protested.

"I'm not an invalid." He didn't bother hiding his annoyance. "I'll fix the leaky pipe, and then we'll all go to the store together."

There was a long pause before she finally relented. "If you insist. I guess I could pick up a few things, myself." Kayla finished eating as Shelby stood and began clearing the dishes. "Leave them, Shelby. Would you mind going out with the kids to bring in more firewood from the woodpile?"

"Sure, after I finish with the dishes." Shelby cleared off the rest of the dishes, neatly stacking them next to the sink, until Kayla stopped her.

"Please? I hate bringing in the firewood and Brianna loves to do it," Kayla said. "I'm sure Cody will get a kick out of helping, too. They could use a break from being indoors, give them a chance to play in the snow. If you'd supervise, I'd be grateful."

"All right then." Shelby finished clearing the dishes and then took the kids and the puppy into the great room, so they could put their coats and boots on.

Alex stayed where he was for a minute, wrestling his frustration under control. How was he going to get back into the field if he couldn't fix a leaky pipe? "I'm not helpless," he told Kayla.

Kayla finished her food and took her plate to the

sink, her back stiff. She filled the sink full of warm soapy water and began scrubbing. There was a distinctive dripping sound as water fell into a bucket beneath the sink. "I never said you were. But if you slip and hurt your hand worse…"

"Kay." He stood and crossed over to her, turning her shoulders so that she faced him, ignoring the sudsy water that dripped to the floor. "If I can reinjure my hand by fixing a leaky pipe, my career is over."

"So what? Would that be the worst thing in the world?" she burst out in exasperation. "Alex, you have a son now, a responsibility—" Her voice cut off and she sighed.

"Kayla," he began, but she quickly interrupted.

"I promised myself I wouldn't harp, but Alex, be reasonable. You know as well as I do your career isn't conducive to raising a family. And now that you know about Cody, you can't simply abandon him. He needs you."

"Give me some credit, Kay. I know I have a son and believe me, he is my primary concern. But don't you see? To keep him safe, I need to finish this case. And the only way to get back to work is to strengthen my left hand."

She let out a heavy sigh. "Can't your partner, that coast guard guy, handle the case? You've already been stabbed. You're lucky to be alive. Isn't that enough?"

"No, Rafe can't finish this case alone. He needs me. And I need to be able to close this case." And afterward? He didn't even want to think about what might happen then. What would he do? How would he find a way to keep drugs off the streets? And how would he learn to be a father to Cody?

Kayla rolled her eyes in disgust. "Fine. Go ahead and

put your life on the line, then. Cody's already lost his mother, who cares if he loses his father, too?"

Please bless my other dad.

Cody's prayer reverberated through his mind. But he steeled his resolve. He couldn't give up the case. Not now. Not until they'd brought the mastermind behind the drug smuggling operation to justice.

"Go help Shelby with the firewood," Kayla said in a resigned tone. She clearly didn't want to discuss the matter any further. "I'm sure the kids will be no help, since they'll be covered in snow."

Before he could move, Shelby burst through the doorway, her eyes wide with alarm.

"Alex! I need you to come outside right away." Her hands were shaking and her face was chalk white.

"What's wrong?" He crossed over to her in two steps.

"I found footprints and a tiny pile of cigarette butts in the snow behind the woodpile. I—I think someone was out here, watching us."

SIX

"Show me," Alex commanded. Shelby didn't bother to argue, quickly leading the way outside, clenching her teeth together to keep them from chattering.

"Right here," she said, pointing to a small area a few feet behind the woodpile, between two rather large oak trees. It wasn't exactly the same place she'd seen the light, but it was close. "I know you're going to think I'm crazy but I found them because of the smell."

He sent her a questioning look. "There's only a couple of cigarette butts here."

She lifted a shoulder, helplessly. "I still smelled them."

This wasn't the time, or the place to explain how the slightest scent of cigarette smoke made her gag, ever since she'd been attacked by the shipyard by some man who'd reeked of cigarettes.

Sometimes, she could still smell the stench of stale cigarette smoke in her dreams. Today when she'd gotten close to the woodpile, she thought she was imagining things.

But then she found footprints. And cigarette butts.

Alex approached the area, crouched down and looked

at the telltale evidence preserved in the snow, his expression intent. He glanced up at her when the kids came running outside to get another armload of firewood.

"Shelby, get the kids back inside the house. Now."

She understood his concern and turned, pasting a smile on her face. "Cody, Brianna. It's time to go inside."

"No! We don't wanna go in!" Cody's tone was belligerent.

"Cody, don't argue," she said in a sharp, no-nonsense tone. The one she used to make him understand she was not kidding. "Inside the house. Now."

For a moment he stared at her defiantly, but when she kept her expression seriously stern, he grudgingly complied. Brianna followed without a protest.

"Take Clyde with you," Shelby added. She was thankful when Kayla met the kids at the door, to help with their wet clothes. Alex's sister cast a worried glance in their direction, but Shelby didn't know how to reassure her.

What if Cody's bad man had found them? The idea that she might have put Kayla and Brianna in danger by coming here made her feel sick to her stomach.

Fighting to control the panic that threatened to overwhelm her, she turned back to Alex. He was working as if she weren't there, following the path of boot-prints as they wove their way through the trees, toward the back of the far side of the house. The opposite side from where the shed was.

He stopped in another clearing and looked up at the house. She followed his gaze, trying to gauge the layout of the upper story. She hoped it was one of the empty rooms, and not hers or Cody's.

The wind kicked up, dark clouds swirling overhead, bringing a threat of more snow. The sky turned an eerie gray-green. She shivered, from cold and fear.

"Come inside," Alex said in a low tone as he headed toward the front door.

The house was blessedly warm and they could hear Kayla's voice in the kitchen as she entertained the kids. Sounded like she was trying to find dry clothes for Cody to wear.

Alex swiftly shed his outer gear and went straight up the stairs to the second story living quarters. Full of curious dread, she followed him.

He stood in Cody's room, gazing out the patio doors. When she came up beside him, she could easily see the indentations in the snow where the cigarette smoker had stood and watched the house.

Watched Cody.

Shelby glanced at Alex as he abruptly swung away from the window. He muttered something unintelligible under his breath and reached for his phone.

"Rafe? I need backup, ASAP."

She imagined his coast guard contact had readily agreed because Alex listened and then said, "Get in touch with Holden first, ask what's going on with Trina's murder investigation and then get here as fast as you can," before snapping his phone shut.

"Do we really need him to come here?" she asked, wishing they could handle this on their own, without involving anyone else. "Can't we all just leave?"

Alex scowled and shook his head. "I can't be responsible for keeping everyone safe. I haven't been officially cleared to return to duty. I should have turned you and Cody over to Rafe from the beginning."

"I'm glad you didn't."

He pinned her with a narrow gaze. "Really? Because I got the distinct impression last night that you couldn't get away from me fast enough. It's obvious you don't trust me."

"I trust you." She was surprised to realize it was true. Despite her irrational fear last night, when she'd felt crowded and let her haunted memories of the past get the better of her, she did trust Alex. Far more than she trusted anyone else.

Including the unknown Rafe.

He let out a harsh laugh. "Yeah, right. Why would you trust me? You told me you saw a light last night, but I didn't take the threat seriously enough."

"You investigated," she protested.

"Yeah, I did. And I checked behind the woodpile and didn't see these footprints, so they must have been made after I came inside. But still, when I didn't see anyone outside, I should have called Rafe for backup."

She didn't know what to say to that. If Rafe had been there helping Alex, would they have found the guy? Maybe. But maybe it would have led to another confrontation where someone got shot, or even killed. There was no way to know.

Self-recrimination blazed in his eyes before he turned away. "My negligence nearly got you and Cody killed."

She didn't believe that, not for a moment, but she also couldn't deny how seeing those footprints in the snow along with the two cigarette butts had shaken her deeply.

"How did he find us?" she asked, bewildered.

"I don't know. But it doesn't really matter, since we're not staying here." Alex turned and stalked toward the door. "Pack up whatever you have and borrow stuff from Kayla if necessary. Rafe should be here within the hour."

Alex had arranged what he could as far as next steps in his escape plan. When those preparations were finished, he began working on Kayla's leaky pipe, since standing around and waiting was driving him crazy.

Rafe arrived fifteen minutes later. Alex heard Rafe and Kayla talking in the great room. No doubt his sister was filling Rafe in on the details of what had happened before Rafe came to find him.

"Alex. Is it true?" his coast guard partner demanded.

"What? That I blew it last night?" He snorted and nodded. "Yeah, I'm afraid it is."

Rafe sent an exasperated glance. "Not that. The boy. Cody. Is he really your son?"

He concentrated on wielding the bulky pipe wrench with his left hand, ignoring the zinging pain that traveled up his right arm. He thought about how he'd planned to have a DNA test, but it wasn't necessary. He knew, with deep certainty, Cody was his son. He finished opening up the elbow pipe and lowered the wrench, sitting back on his heels. "Yes. It's true. He's a good kid, but a scared one. He saw something the night before Trina was shot."

"Something? Like what? Didn't you talk to him?"

"He's only four, Rafe. I can't very well interrogate him." Odd how he sounded like Shelby when she'd staunchly defended Cody. "He's been traumatized, practically saw his mother being killed. Besides, it's not as if the court is going to take action on the word of a child eyewitness."

"Maybe not the court, but it would give us something to go on," Rafe responded. "We need answers and we need them quickly."

"I know." He went back to work on the pipe. "I will talk to him, later. Right now, I want you to get a security system installed here at the B & B."

"A security system, are you crazy? Your sister and her daughter can't stay here," Rafe argued hotly. "Not until we've cracked this case."

"I know, but I want it installed anyway, for when they can return."

Rafe looked like he was going to argue, not that Alex could blame him. What good would a security system do if Kayla's business involved inviting strangers into her home on a regular basis? He didn't care. He didn't want an intruder on the grounds catching him or Kayla unaware ever again.

"Okay, consider it done. Anything else?" Rafe asked.

He'd made a lot of arrangements, but he wasn't sure Rafe was going to approve. Especially since he wasn't quite ready to turn over Shelby and Cody into Rafe's protection. He lifted the heavy wrench again. "I've made some initial plans," he admitted.

"Like what?"

He glanced at Rafe and in the split second he'd taken his eye off the pipe, the wrench slipped from his grasp. Since he was leaning on it with all his strength, the tool skipped off the pipe and crashed back down on his injured right hand landing directly on the deepest and longest surgical scar.

Blood spurted from the wound and a shaft of pain stole his breath, as if he'd been hit by a cargo flat full of steel. For a moment he was paralyzed by the pain.

When the dizziness passed, he scrambled to his feet, holding his injured arm and swallowing the waves of pain that rolled up his arm. Blood sprayed everywhere, and he vainly attempted to use his other hand to keep it from going all over Kayla's floor.

Cody chose that moment to charge into the kitchen, skidding to a stop, his eyes wide with horror as they fixed on Alex's bloodstained arm.

Alex found his voice. "It's okay, Cody," he hastened to reassure him, forcing a grim smile. "I'm fine. This is no big deal, it's just a scratch."

To his utter surprise, Cody let out a shrill scream. Before Alex could stop him, he turned and ran from the room.

Shelby gasped when she heard Cody scream. She ran into the dining room, snagging him as he darted past. When he saw it was her, he clung like a monkey around her neck.

"Cody, honey, what's wrong?" She gathered him close, running a soothing hand over his back as he trembled and sobbed against her. "Shh, don't cry. You're safe. Don't worry, everything is going to be okay."

Alex came rushing out, a towel wrapped around his right arm. Deep grooves of pain lined his mouth, but he leveled his concerned gaze on Cody.

"Is he okay?" Alex asked.

She shook her head, feeling helpless. What had

gotten Cody so riled up? He'd seen small injuries before at the daycare. They'd never upset him like this. "What happened in there?"

"I'm not sure." Alex tightened his grip on the towel.

Shelby held Cody until he stopped crying, realizing the young boy's emotional status was more fragile than she'd realized. He needed to talk to a professional child psychologist, the sooner the better.

Kayla walked up behind her. "You'd better let me take a look at that," she said, indicating his injured arm.

Alex frowned and shook his head. "Later. I think Cody freaked out because of the blood."

Why would Cody react so strongly to the sight of blood? She continued to hold him close, murmuring words of encouragement even as her mind raced over the possibilities.

He couldn't have seen blood from Trina being shot, because his mother and the gunman had been too far away. She hadn't even seen any blood, and she was the one who saw Trina drop to the ground.

Which meant Cody had to have seen blood at another time. Like when he saw his mother talking to the bad man. Had he witnessed a physical confrontation? Trina hadn't seemed injured when she'd handed over Cody at the marina, so perhaps she'd hit the bad man so she could escape.

Alex's green gaze was watching her intently and she wondered if he'd come to the same conclusions she had. She narrowed her gaze, vowing to monitor Alex's questions for Cody very careful. Yes, they needed the information, but there had to be away for getting it from Cody without upsetting him further. If the poor child reacted like this to the sight of blood, then he'd been far more traumatized by what he'd seen than she'd imagined.

"I'm going to take him upstairs for a minute," she murmured, hitching Cody higher in her arms so she could carry him through the great room.

She half expected Alex to stop her, but he didn't. She could feel his gaze boring into her back as she headed upstairs to the sanctuary of their rooms.

After she'd gotten Cody calmed down and had washed the tears from his face, they returned to the kitchen where Rafe, Kayla and Alex were gathered around the large picnic table. She was relieved to see that a bulky white bandage covered Alex's injured arm.

"I don't understand why I have to go anywhere," Kayla was saying in a stubborn tone. "I'm fine with you taking Brianna someplace safe, with Ellen, my mother-in-law, to watch, but there's no reason for me to leave, too."

Alex opened his mouth to argue, but Rafe beat him to it.

"No. Absolutely not. You will be safe. I won't allow anything else," Rafe commanded, anxiety making his thick Hispanic accent stronger.

"You won't allow it?" Kayla narrowed her gaze. "You don't have control over what I do."

"The decision has been made," Rafe brushed aside her protest as if it was nothing more than a bug to be squashed. "You, Brianna and her grandmother will enjoy an extended stay at a resort offering an indoor water park for entertainment."

"Why drag Ellen into this?" Kayla asked.

"Because your mother-in-law was watching Brianna the day Shelby arrived. If someone had followed her, we can't assume they didn't see Ellen dropping Brianna off later that day. I don't want to take a chance on her safety."

When it looked like Kayla was going to argue some more, Shelby stepped in, catching Kayla's gaze with hers. "Please go somewhere safe. For me? I hate knowing I put you and Brianna in danger by coming here."

"It's not your fault, Shelby." Kayla's stout defense touched her heart. "But if you think I should go, I will." Her eyes widened and she glanced at her brother. "Maybe Cody should come with us?"

Considering the magnitude of Cody's breakdown, Shelby didn't think leaving him alone with Kayla and Brianna was a good idea at all. "I don't think so…"

Rafe and Alex exchanged a look and they both simultaneously shook their heads. Alex spoke up. "No, Cody needs Shelby."

She was pleased he'd understood. Obviously Alex really did have Cody's best interests at heart.

"I've made arrangements for Shelby and me to hide out in a small hotel several miles from here," Alex said, changing the subject. "Rafe, I want you to take Kayla, Brianna and her grandmother to the resort and then come and meet up with us afterward."

Rafe nodded. "All right. But I think we need to get rid of Shelby's car, in case someone used it to track her here. I can't figure out how else they found her. I tried checking it over, but without the proper instruments, a tracking device could be anywhere. I thought I'd have some friends of mine pick it up and take it back to Green Bay."

"Sounds reasonable." Alex raised a brow. "Can I borrow your Jeep? There's a storm headed this way."

"Sure."

They finalized their plans. Kayla offered the use of her SUV since Ellen had agreed to pick up her and Brianna to head to the resort. When they had every angle covered, they ate some quickly prepared sandwiches, more for the kids' sake, before splitting up.

When Cody realized the puppy wasn't coming with them, he threw a rare temper tantrum. Shelby concentrated on calming him down, and she couldn't help wondering if she'd made the right decision. Was she being selfish? Would it be better for Cody to be at the water park resort with Kayla and Brianna?

"Did you know that Clyde is going to have a new batch of brothers and sisters soon?" Alex asked, crouching down so he was at eye level with Cody.

Magically the boy's tears vanished. "Really?"

Alex gave a solemn nod. "Yep, the puppies are due in early May. Maybe we can get one of the puppies for you. Would you like that?"

Cody's eyes widened in awe. "A puppy? For my very own?"

Shelby wanted to protest that Alex had no right to promise such a thing, yet hadn't she already thought of getting Cody a puppy once this was over? Still, this was the sort of thing both parents should agree on. Alex had no idea she'd planned on allowing Cody to have a pet.

"You have to be a good boy and listen to your mother—er—your aunt Shelby. Do you understand?"

Cody nodded vigorously and the crisis was adverted.

Irrationally annoyed, the brief conversation replayed over and over in her mind as she buckled Cody's toddler seat into the back of Rafe's Jeep.

"All set?" Alex asked softly.

She nodded and pushed her uncharitable thoughts away. Why was she upset? This was what she'd wanted, for Cody and Alex to have some sort of relationship. She'd asked for God's help. He'd answered. She should be glad.

She then buckled Cody in, making sure he had his animal kingdom figures to help keep him entertained on the long ride, before she climbed into the passenger seat. The time was only about three in the afternoon, but the clouds were so dark and thick overhead that the hour seemed much later.

She swallowed hard, trying not to succumb to the impending sense of doom. Being close to Alex in the car was a bit unnerving. She wasn't afraid of him, but it felt strange for her and Cody to be alone with him. Still, she couldn't deny she was relieved they were leaving the bed-and-breakfast and those disturbing cigarette butts, to find anonymity in another hotel far from here.

"Do you really think the bad guy put something on my car?" she asked.

He glanced at her, his brow furrowed in a deep frown. "I'm not sure how they found you, Shelby. Could be they somehow tracked either Trina's phone or your car. Or maybe you were followed and we just didn't catch on. But either way, we should have our bases covered now. You didn't bring Trina's phone, right?"

"I turned it off and left it back at the B & B like you told me to do."

"Good. I'm sure we'll be fine."

He sounded so certain, she believed him. Slowly she unclenched her twisted hands, willing herself to relax.

Alex had only driven for ten miles when large, fat,

wet snowflakes began to fall. The slick roads forced him to slow his speed considerably.

"Do you think we'll get to the hotel before dinnertime?" she asked, not because she was hungry but because traveling with a child Cody's age meant keeping track of meals.

"I hope so." Alex's attention was riveted on the highway. She could see from the compass in Rafe's Jeep they were heading northeast.

The snow fell harder, covering the roads with an icy slush, forcing Alex to slow his speed even further. He glanced in the rearview mirror frequently.

"Is there someone behind us?" Shelby asked, craning her neck around.

"Yeah. For the past two miles." Alex did not look happy and he gripped the steering wheel tightly. "As soon as I find a cross street, I'm going to pull off so we can lose him."

Her stomach clenched. Another coincidence? She hoped so.

"What is he doing?" Alex suddenly ground out.

Before she could ask what he meant, she saw the black truck swerve into the oncoming lane of traffic, pulling up beside them even though they were in a no-passing zone, heading into a sharp curve in the highway.

"Hang on!" Alex shouted as he hit the brakes.

Too late. The black truck smashed into them, sending the Jeep skidding across the slick road, crashing up against the side rail of the highway.

"No!" Shelby cried. The metal rail gave away, allowing the Jeep to barrel down into the steep ravine below.

SEVEN

Alex fought to stay conscious, even though his head pounded from the impact of the air-bag deployment. The Jeep finally came to rest against a band of evergreens, miraculously intact. For long moments he couldn't move. The abrupt silence after listening to the Jeep crash against the rocks and trees was just as deafening.

"Shelby?" He leaned over to put a hand on her shoulder, fearing the worst. Relief overwhelmed him when she stirred and lifted her head. There was a small cut on her forehead, but her eyes were clear.

"I'm fine. Cody?"

Cody, who didn't have the benefit of air bags to protect him from the crash. Alarm gripped him by the throat and he struggled to release the latch of the seat belt so he could turn around to check his son.

A soft keening cry from the backseat nearly made him weep in relief. Shelby got her seat belt undone first and crammed her body through the narrow opening between the seats to reach him.

"Shh, Cody. It's all right. We're fine. God was watching over us. He kept us safe."

Alex paused at her words. Maybe she was right.

Maybe God had been watching over them. This accident could have ended much worse.

Except it wasn't an accident. The black truck had stayed on his tail, no matter how hard he'd tried to put distance between them. And when the truck had pulled up alongside, Alex had glimpsed the driver through the tinted windows the moment the guy had jerked the steering wheel, sideswiping them.

There was no doubt in his mind that the driver of the black truck had hit them on purpose. Alex would have bet his pension on it. Spurred by a new sense of urgency, he unlatched his seat belt and took stock of their situation. Thankfully they'd taken Rafe's sturdy Jeep. If they'd been in Shelby's small compact car, they wouldn't have stood much of a chance. He swallowed hard, trying to see out the cracked window.

The snow had cushioned their fall, minimizing the damage but they weren't out of danger yet. The driver of the black truck could be right now coming down the ravine to finish what he'd started.

"We can't stay here," he rasped, using all his strength to pry his dented driver's door open.

Shelby had gotten Cody out of his seat and was holding him protectively in her arms. "Alex, it's cold and wet out there. He'll freeze."

He shared her concern. Cody's body mass was so small he was at a much higher risk for hypothermia. Yet if they stayed here, they were too much like a beacon, drawing the driver of the truck directly toward them.

"I'll come up with something," he promised before he jumped out into the snow and made his way to the back of the Jeep.

Rafe worked for the coast guard. And he loved to camp and fish. Surely he had some leftover gear in the back they could use. The back window was broken open and he leaned in, thrilled to discover his gut instincts were right.

Rafe had plenty of stuff tossed back there.

As he rummaged through the gear, picking and choosing what they needed the most and discarding the items that held little value other than weighing them down, he listened to Shelby talking in a low voice to Cody.

No, not talking. Praying.

"Heavenly Father, we thank You for keeping us safe in Your loving arms. Please continue to give us Your strength and guidance, Lord, as we seek shelter from the storm. Amen."

Cody's young voice echoed, "Amen."

Humbled, he finished rifling through Rafe's things with a renewed sense of purpose. They could do this. After all, God was watching over Shelby and Cody.

And maybe, even though he hadn't prayed or stepped inside anything resembling a church in years, God was watching over him, too.

Alex climbed back into the Jeep with his loot of supplies. He knew Shelby had doubts about the wisdom of leaving the vehicle.

She phrased her next words carefully. "Won't it be better to stay here, until we're rescued?"

"We don't want just anyone to find us," he answered, with a meaningful glance at Cody. Her eyes widened when she absorbed his hidden meaning. "Don't worry," he interjected when she opened her mouth. "We won't have to hike too far. As soon as we're safely hidden, I'll get in touch with Rafe."

"Cody is too young to hike," she protested.

"I'm going to make a sling, like this, and carry Cody against my chest. Rafe has a survival blanket which helps contain body heat. With the survival blanket and sharing my body heat, he'll be as snug as a bug in a rug."

He was encouraged when she forced a smile and nodded. "Sounds like a plan."

Considering it was the only plan he had at the moment, he didn't respond. Hiking through the snow while carrying Cody's additional weight would not be easy. He'd made the sling out of the nylon tent, but Shelby would have to carry a pack of supplies, too. When he handed her the gear, she didn't voice a single complaint.

Soon they were ready to go.

Outside, he scanned the area, searching for any sign that the driver of the black truck was making his way to find them. But the swirling snow had a negative impact on the visibility and the only sound he could hear was the whistling wind.

As much as he would have preferred taking the easy route using gravity to head farther down the ravine, he forced himself to take a parallel path from the Jeep, going back in the direction from which they'd come.

He wasn't crazy, he simply hoped to buy a little time, in case his worst fears were correct and the driver was brave enough or foolish enough to search for them. With any luck, by the time the guy found the Jeep, partially hidden in the evergreen trees, the wind would have obliterated their tracks in the snow. The driver would assume that since they had Cody, they'd head down the ravine, continuing north.

It wasn't a perfect plan, but the best he could drum up at the moment.

As if sensing the seriousness of the situation, Cody kept quiet in his makeshift sling. Alex tried to keep his gait as smooth as possible, clasping one arm securely around the boy to avoid jostling him too much. He led the way, but had insisted he and Shelby be tied together with rope found in the back of Rafe's Jeep, since they could barely see a few feet in front of their faces.

He'd figured they'd only gone about a mile when the rope tugged sharply. He stopped and turned around to find Shelby on her hands and knees in the snow. He staggered toward her, a sense of hopelessness washing over him.

How much more could Shelby take? They'd barely gone a mile but in these adverse conditions, it seemed like ten. He was breathing hard and he was accustomed to physical labor. How much longer could they battle the storm? They needed shelter. Soon.

He helped Shelby to her feet, and clasped her hands, peering at her through the snow. "Are you all right?"

Her mouth trembled but she nodded. "Fine," she whispered.

Encouraged, he gave her hands a gentle squeeze before letting go. He turned about to face the invisible path he'd chosen.

As he walked, his boots sinking as far as his knees in some places, portions of Shelby's prayer echoed in his mind and he found himself repeating them over and over again.

Heavenly Father, show us the way. Give us Your strength and guidance. Keep us safe.

Shelby clenched her teeth together, trying to keep them from clattering. Alex was amazing. He'd managed to rig up the tent he'd used to carry Cody into a temporary shelter between two large fir trees. Then he'd spread out another tarp over the snow-covered ground to minimize the chill. She was grateful he'd kept the survival blanket around Cody. With the shelter overhead and the trees around them, they were safe from the snow and the wind, but she was still wet and cold.

He'd used his cell phone to contact Rafe. At first she'd been worried the storm would ruin their connection but texting worked perfectly. They'd arranged for Rafe to contact them again, once he was in the general location, so Alex could risk marking their location with a flare.

"Here, you hold Cody for a while," he said in a low voice, noticing her shivers despite her attempts to hide the extent of her discomfort.

"No, I don't want him to get chilled." She stuck her icy hands under her armpits, shivering at the coldness. "He'll be warmer with you."

"He'll be okay. He's drier than we are and with that survival blanket around him, his body is literally radiating heat." She was grateful Cody appeared to be sleeping, a natural sleep, not one from dangerous hypothermia. Alex glanced at her. "You'll need to take him soon anyway, when Rafe arrives."

"I'll wait until then." When the feeling in her fingers returned, she clasped her knees to her chest, hugging them close. She wanted to ask if Rafe would get here soon, but there was no point in asking the impossible. In this weather, it could easily take him hours.

She closed her eyes, giving in to her numbing exhaustion.

"Shelby," Alex said, shaking her to get her attention. "Stay awake. Here, come over next to me, I have enough body heat for the both of us."

Gratefully, she scooted closer, leaning against him. He wrapped his arm around her, hugging her close. He was right. She could already feel some of his warmth seeping through her jacket.

"Don't go to sleep," he commanded softly, still keeping his voice low so as not to disturb Cody. "Talk to me."

"Talk? About what?"

"Anything." He rubbed her arm, helping to warm the side of her that wasn't pressed against his warmth. "Tell me about yourself. What made you decide to open a day care center?"

Since that was actually a fairly long story, she decided to give him the abbreviated version. "I majored in education in college with a minor in business. I taught fifth grade for a while, but it wasn't exactly what I was looking for. After Cody was born, it seemed natural to open a day care center."

"Natural? What do you mean?"

"Teaching was all right, but I wanted more. I discovered I'm able to make a bigger impact in my children's lives through the day care center."

"I'm sure you've made a huge impact on Cody's life," Alex murmured. "He's a great kid."

"Thank you." She smiled, finding it was easy to talk in the cozy darkness. If not for being so chilled, she'd be comfortable here with Alex. "Yes, I like to think I'm making a difference. Trina and Stephan were very busy managing the marina. I often kept Cody overnight in my apartment above the day care. I used to wonder why they didn't spend more time with him, but now that I know Stephan knew he wasn't Cody's father, it makes sense. Although I still think Trina should have been more of a mother to Cody. I guess she was trying to make Stephan happy, too."

"Stephan wasn't—mean to him, was he?"

"No," she hastily reassured him. "More like indifferent in a way. I just thought they were always too busy to make time for him."

"So you really have been like a mother to him." He paused and then added, "Didn't you ever think about having a family of your own?"

"I'd love to have children some day." She couldn't hide the longing in her tone. She stared into the darkness, thinking it was funny how she wasn't afraid to be with Alex like this. "But I guess you've probably realized I have issues. With men."

"All men?" he probed gently. "Not just me?"

"All men." She felt bad he'd taken her aversion personally. "Unfortunately, I was attacked twice. The first time was a near miss in college." She had no idea why she was telling him all of this, when she normally preferred not to talk about the attacks at all.

"What do you mean by a near miss?" This time his tone was lined with steel. "Did some jerk hurt you? Did he—?"

"No." She couldn't let him think the worst, and tried to downplay what had happened, as if she hadn't been completely terrorized at the time. "He didn't want to take no for an answer, but I managed to get away, mostly unscathed."

"Mostly unscathed." There was a strange undertone in his voice, one she couldn't quite pin down.

"A few bruises, nothing more." She turned her head in the darkness, trying to see him, wishing she could read the expression in his eyes.

"Bruises." There was a tense silence. "And the second time?"

"I was attacked down at the shipyard."

She thought he tensed beside her, but when he didn't say anything, she continued.

"A man came up behind me and grabbed me. I thought he was going to drag me into the warehouse, but he hit me over the head. I woke up in the hospital, and they said I was only physically attacked, nothing more." At the time she'd feared the worst, that she'd been sexually assaulted while she was unconscious. But even without that violation, the two attacks had sometimes blurred into one awful nightmare where she'd been unable to get away. Her fear colored her interactions with every man she'd dealt with ever since.

There was another long pause. "Did they arrest the man who hit you?"

"No." She'd often wondered if that was part of the reason she remained so haunted by the attacks. She'd sought solace in God, but there was still a part of her that was worried the man who'd attacked her would find her again.

"You reported the jerk in college, didn't you?"

She couldn't answer. Because she had, but the entire

event had turned into a fiasco to the point where she was made to feel like the guilty one. After all, she'd agreed to meet him in his dorm room. And he had claimed that she led him on, then changed her mind. The bruises on her chest and arms hadn't convinced the authorities to press charges.

That experience, along with the attack at the shipyard made her want to protect Cody from being a victim, too.

Alex's phone beeped, indicating a new text message. He looked at the message, and then shut the phone.

"Rafe is on the road where we went over. Take Cody so I can set the flare."

"All right." She gladly took the burden of Cody's weight. The boy roused a bit with the movement.

Alex pulled the flare out of his coat pocket and made his way to the edge of their enclosure.

"Shelby?" She glanced up at him. "We're not finished with this conversation."

Before she could respond, he disappeared into the cold.

She huddled with Cody, missing Alex's warm presence. Somehow, being with him, the two of them caring for Cody, felt right. Sharing her secrets with Alex hadn't been as difficult as she'd imagined.

She was starting to care for him.

And that thought scared her more than being caught in the middle of a snowstorm.

Alex didn't completely relax until he'd gotten Shelby and Cody safely tucked into Kayla's SUV which Rafe had brought to pick them up.

That had been a close call. Too close. If they hadn't had Rafe's Jeep, complete with the camping supplies in the back, there was a very good chance they would have died from hypothermia exposure before Rafe had been able to rescue them.

Had that been the truck driver's plan?

Alex had to believe it was. He'd given Rafe all the details leading up to their crash and Rafe agreed that, somehow, the smoker who'd been watching outside the bed-and-breakfast had followed them.

The roads were still in bad shape, so it took them longer than planned to reach the small motel, located in the middle of a dinky town that was nothing but a speck on most road maps.

"I'll order something to eat," Alex said, after they'd secured two connecting rooms. "At least there's a small café attached, or we'd really be in trouble."

Shelby nodded, looking relieved to have decent living quarters after the time they'd spent in a makeshift tent. He guessed she was still chilled when she'd immediately crossed the room to crank up the heat.

"Keep the connecting door unlocked, would you?" he asked. "Rafe and I will be right next door. We'll let you know when the pizza arrives."

"Sure," she said with an exhausted smile.

"Maybe we should take shifts staying on guard tonight," Rafe suggested in a low tone after they'd left Shelby and Cody alone. "Just in case."

"You're probably right, although I don't see how we could have been followed," Alex said with a sigh. "There wasn't another soul behind us once we got off the main highway. This town isn't exactly a hot spot."

"I know, but I still don't like it that you were followed at all," Rafe said with a scowl.

He didn't like it, either. "You arranged to have Shelby's car returned to Green Bay?"

Rafe nodded. "Everything worked out fine. Two friends of mine picked up Shelby's car. Kayla, Brianna and Ellen are safe at the resort. I was heading back to Green Bay myself when you called."

"I'm going to get cleaned up a bit," Alex said. "By then the pizza should be here. If you want to take shifts, tonight, that's fine with me."

"I'll take the first shift, since you look like you could use some sleep."

Alex doubted he'd be able to sleep, no matter how exhausted he was. Those moments the black truck had rammed into them would be forever etched in his mind. What if something had happened to Cody? Or Shelby? The thought of either of them being injured, or worse, made him feel sick to his stomach. They'd only been part of his life for a couple of days, but suddenly he couldn't imagine living without them.

He cleaned up in the bathroom and when he emerged ten minutes later, he could smell the enticing scent of pizza. Rafe and Shelby were speaking in low tones in the room next door.

When he stepped through the connecting door, he abruptly stopped, surprised to see Rafe, Shelby and Cody, all sitting with their heads bowed, as Rafe prayed.

"Dear Lord, thank You for providing us food to eat and shelter from the storm. We are grateful to have You watching over us and providing for us. Amen."

Awkwardly, he stood and waited for them to finish before coming farther into the room. He and Rafe had been partners over the past few years while working this case, but it wasn't as if they'd spent a lot of time together, considering he'd been deep undercover as a longshoreman. He'd seen the simple gold cross Rafe wore like a talisman around his neck, but Alex had figured it was more for decoration rather than as a true symbol of Rafe's religious beliefs.

Obviously, he'd been wrong.

After they finished the pizza, Alex cleaned up the mess while Shelby tucked Cody into bed. Rafe went outside to do a perimeter check around the hotel area to make sure there was nothing suspicious. Alex stood in the entryway between their rooms, watching as Cody finished up his prayers.

He gestured Shelby over when she doused the lamp next to the beds, leaving just the bathroom light on.

"What is it?" she asked.

"Shelby, while Rafe is outside, I want to talk to you. It's important." Alex pulled up two chairs, so they could sit down.

"All right," she agreed, her expression wary. "What is it?"

He took a deep breath, trying to think of a way to tell her. He wanted to say something sooner, when she'd bared her secrets about the attacks but Rafe's arrival had interrupted them.

There was just no easy way to break the news. "I was there that night," he finally said. "At the shipyard. When you were attacked. I happened to be coming toward the warehouse, when I heard something. When I turned to look, I saw the guy grab you."

"You saw him? You can identify him?" The hope in her voice only made him feel worse.

"I wish I could, but his back was toward me and since he was dressed like every other longshoreman with a knit cap pulled over his head, I couldn't tell who he was. But I created a diversion, which was when he hit you and left you there. Once he'd gotten away from you, I called the police. I went over to make sure you were okay, staying by your side until I heard the sirens. I left before the police arrived, so I wouldn't risk blowing my cover."

She gaped at him. "You didn't tell the police what you saw?"

He slowly shook his head. "No. I'm sorry, but I couldn't be seen cooperating with the police. Not when I was trying to behave like the kind of guy who wanted to be included in the action of the drug running operation."

"I see." She dropped her gaze to her hands, twisted tightly in her lap.

"Shelby, I'm so sorry. Please try to understand. If I'd had information that would help the police catch the guy, I would have left an anonymous tip. But I didn't see anything that would help me identify him."

"I understand, really." Shelby's attempt at a smile was pitiful.

"Why did you go down to the warehouse that night?" he asked, puzzled. It had only been a fleeting moment in the middle of his case and he hadn't immediately recognized Shelby as the woman who he'd helped back then.

"I was looking for Trina and my father said she was down at the warehouse."

The warehouse where there were likely hidden drugs. Why would Russ Jacobson send Shelby to the shipyard where rough longshoremen hung out? He stared at her, trying to remember what she'd looked like back then. "You wore your hair shorter, didn't you?"

"Yes. And it was much lighter from being out in the sun."

Realization dawned and he wondered why he hadn't thought of this earlier. "I bet the guy who attacked you mistook you for Trina!"

EIGHT

Shelby stared at Alex, her mind whirling. It was difficult to comprehend that Alex had been there the night of her attack, risking his cover to help her. The idea that he was there, looking out for her while she was unconscious, was oddly reassuring.

But was he right in that the attacker thought she was her sister? Shelby forced herself to go back to that night in her mind, dragging long buried memories to the surface.

She was walking toward the warehouse located at the farthest end of the shipyard. The area was not well lit, several of the overhead lights were burned out. She'd thought she was alone.

The hint of cigarette smoke made her wrinkle her nose. A male voice had called, "Trina?"

She shook her head as she started to turn around to see who'd called her Trina. But the smell of cigarettes got stronger. Hard fingers dug into her arms. Before she could scream, something hard had struck her in the temple. Darkness surrounded her.

She winced a bit, remembering the pain in her head when she'd finally awakened in the hospital, surrounded by medical personnel. The police had been there, asking her over and over again if she'd seen the man who'd attacked her.

She hadn't. But she'd remembered the stench, the thick odor of cigarette smoke. And the bitter taste of fear as she wondered if he'd done anything else to her. Ever since that night, she'd been afraid of the dark, had asked for God's strength to help conquer her fears.

Up until tonight, she hadn't remembered her attacker had called her by her sister's name.

"Shelby?" Alex took hold of her hand, breaking her from her reverie. "Are you all right?"

For a moment she stared at their entwined hands, before raising her eyes to meet his compassionate gaze. "You're right. He did mistake me for Trina at first," she finally admitted. "But I responded seconds before I started to turn around. Just as I caught a glimpse of him, he attacked."

His fingers tightened around hers and the expression in his eyes was full of agony. "I'm sorry I couldn't stop him, Shelby. I'm so sorry."

She tried to smile. "It's okay. The point is that I don't think he attacked me because he thought I was Trina. Quite the opposite. I believe he attacked me because I *wasn't* Trina. Because when he realized who I was, he didn't want me anywhere near the warehouse."

He sucked in a harsh breath. "That makes sense. The minute he knew you weren't Trina, he had to get rid of you to stop you from stumbling into something you shouldn't." His gaze was thoughtful. "I wonder if a big drug shipment was scheduled to come in that night?"

She didn't like the sound of that. "You're telling me they trusted Trina with drug smuggling information?"

she asked, appalled. "That they considered her part of that business?"

"I'm afraid so." Alex's expression was one of chagrined guilt. "You need to know, it was Trina's idea from the very beginning. She was trying to gain their trust, so she could get information about the identity of the drug smugglers. She felt it was the only way to prove your father was innocent."

She wrapped her arms around her stomach, feeling sick. When Alex had told her Trina was feeding the DEA and coast guard information, she hadn't realized exactly what that role had entailed. But the image he painted was all too real.

Trina had been acting like an undercover agent, much like Alex had been.

And now Trina was dead.

"So that's why they killed her," she whispered.

Alex's expression turned grim. "Yes, that's the only explanation that makes sense to me, too."

The sound of the hotel room door opening prevented them from saying anything further. Rafe stepped inside, stomping the snow from his boots.

"I don't think it's snowing much, but the wind is still blowing pretty hard," Rafe informed them. "I made a huge path around the hotel and I didn't see a single soul who was brave enough to be hanging around outside in this weather. I made note of the cars parked here at the hotel, and I'll run them through the computer. But even without that, I think we're safe for the night."

"Thanks, Rafe," Alex said. He turned to Shelby, gesturing to the connecting room. "You'd better get some rest. It's been a long day. We'll come up with some sort of action plan first thing in the morning."

"All right. Good night, Rafe, Alex." She closed the connecting door most of the way to give her some privacy, leaving it unlocked in case of an emergency.

Knowing they were safe at last, sleep should have come easily, but it didn't. Instead she kept thinking about the night she was attacked, the moment she'd turned to look at who'd called her sister's name.

A blurred face hovered on the edges of her memory, but no matter how hard she tried, she couldn't get that momentary glimpse of the man's face to focus.

When Shelby woke up the next morning, the sun was shining brightly through the windows. Rubbing her gritty eyes, she realized with relief the snowstorm was over.

Her gaze sought Cody, but his bed was empty. She scrambled out of bed to search for him, her heart racing.

Of course, she needn't have worried. The connecting door between the rooms was standing ajar and she soon discovered Cody was bonding with Rafe and Alex, putting a pretty big dent into a box of doughnuts, no doubt purchased from the café next door.

"I never get to eat sweets for breakfast," Cody was saying, his mouth full of Boston crème. "Aunt Shelby always says we hav'ta eat healthy." He made the last word sound like something disgusting.

Miffed, she turned away. Ridiculous as it was, she resented having to be the role model parent, while Alex showered Cody with all the fun stuff.

"We would be eating healthy, too, Cody, if we had a stove to cook on," Alex said. "Don't expect this every day. We're only having doughnuts for breakfast as a special treat."

She paused, mollified by his words.

"'Cause we got in a car crash and fell down the hill?" Cody asked.

"Yes, exactly," Alex agreed. "And because you were such a good boy as we walked through the storm to find shelter."

"How come we didn't see any wild animals?" Cody wanted to know.

A wry smile tugged at the corner of her mouth as she listened to Alex's drawn out response. He didn't seem to mind playing the role of father to Cody, and she was happy they were adjusting so quickly to spending time together.

But as she was about to turn away, she hesitated. If she left Cody alone with Alex while she cleaned up, would he take the opportunity to question the boy about what he'd seen the night Trina died?

Alex had promised he wouldn't question Cody without her permission. She'd trusted Alex to keep them safe, and maybe it was time to trust him to keep his word. She silently closed the connecting door and used the few moments of privacy to freshen up in the bathroom.

When she returned twenty minutes later, feeling much better, she joined the men in the next room.

"What's the plan?" she asked, saying a quick prayer of thanks before she helped herself to the last doughnut. She was very grateful to have something to put in her stomach. "Where are we going from here?"

Alex's expression was serious, as he turned to her. "Do you think it would be okay for Cody to watch cartoons for a while?" he asked.

The doughnut sank like a rock to the bottom of her stomach. Whatever they needed to discuss, Alex didn't want Cody around to hear it.

"Sure. Are you finished eating, Cody?"

"Yeah." He wiped his hands on his pants and she hid a wince.

"All right, let's go find the cartoon channel for a while, okay?" She led Cody back to their room and turned on the television for him. When he was settled in, she returned to Alex and Rafe.

"He doesn't usually watch much TV so I don't know how long the cartoons will hold his attention," she warned.

. The two men exchanged a solemn glance. "Sit down, then. There's some new information that you need to know."

Truly worried now, she sat. "What is it? What's going on?"

Alex leaned forward. "We got some information from Logan Quail, he's the DEA agent that was sent in to help replace me when I was shot."

She frowned. "I thought you said it was too late, that no one could replace you?"

"No one could replace Alex's undercover role," Rafe corrected. "Or his knowledge of the case after all this time. But we did get Logan to help keep an eye on things. He's not undercover in the shipyard as a long-shoreman, but he has managed to get a job in the local packing plant nearby."

She supposed that did make some sense. With Alex recovering, the DEA needed to have someone stationed in Green Bay.

"Logan called first thing this morning with some disturbing news," Alex continued. "Your father's foreman has been found dead."

"Bobby Drake is dead?" She paled. "What happened?"

Rafe shrugged. "Looks like it could be suicide, but we won't know until the ME finishes his report. Suicide or murder, either way, we suspect his death is related to the case."

Alex glanced at her. "And just so you know, there's another weird piece of the puzzle. Your stepmother moved out of your father's house."

"Marilyn?" She raised a brow. "Moved out? Are you sure? I just spoke to her the other day."

"When?" Alex's tone was sharp.

"The first day I arrived at the bed-and-breakfast. Don't glare at me like that, I told you I called my father. Marilyn answered the phone."

Alex scrubbed a hand over his face and softened his tone. "You're right, that is strange. Rafe, tell her exactly what Logan said."

"Logan heard that Russ Jacobson had stormed into to the police station, claiming that Marilyn was missing. A good portion of her personal items were gone, too, but he claimed that she wouldn't have left him voluntarily." Rafe spread his hands wide. "After reviewing the evidence, the police felt differently."

Her poor father. She and Trina hadn't gotten along very well with their stepmother, but they'd accepted her into the family, regardless. Now she'd moved out? It didn't make much sense.

"That doesn't sound like Marilyn," Shelby mused. "To leave like that. I mean, she and my father have been married for nearly five years. She wasn't my favorite person in the world, but as a couple, they seemed to get along well enough. And she certainly enjoyed spending his money."

Alex's expression grew grim. "Shelby, you need to know there have been a lot of rumors over the past few months. About your stepmother's infidelity."

Her eyes widened. "You mean she's cheating on my father?"

Rafe shrugged. "Maybe. It's only a rumor at this point, but it does appear incriminating that she suddenly moved out of your father's house. Some people have suggested she was having an affair with Bobby Drake."

"I thought you said he was dead?"

"He is, but it's possible he killed himself over her. Could be she broke off things with him and took up with someone else."

"Bobby Drake doesn't seem to be her type," she protested. "She likes spending money."

First her father had lost Trina and now his wife. How was he holding up? She remembered how different he'd sounded on the phone, as if the weight of the world rested on his shoulders. "I should be there for him," she murmured.

"It's too dangerous to go back," Alex reminded her gently. "Right now, keeping Cody safe is our main concern."

He was right, she knew it. But the thought of her father dealing with all of this alone ripped her heart into tiny pieces.

"There's a death notice in this morning's paper for Trina," Rafe said, breaking into the prolonged silence.

"Her funeral service is scheduled in three days, for this upcoming Thursday."

"I really want to be there for the funeral," she said.

"I don't think that's a good idea—" Alex started, but she quickly cut him off.

"It's important," she insisted. "For me, my father and for Cody."

Especially for Cody, who deserved the chance to say goodbye to his mother one last time.

"Don't," Rafe said, grabbing Alex's arm to prevent him from following Shelby as she stalked off to the connecting hotel room. "You're not going to talk her out of this one, my friend."

Alex sat down with a heavy sigh, wishing there was some way to make Shelby see reason. "Why is she being so stubborn? It's too dangerous to go back, even for a funeral."

"Would you miss Kayla's funeral?" Rafe asked reasonably.

No, he wouldn't. "That's different," he protested weakly. "There's not someone after me. Besides, Kayla and I are very close."

Rafe raised a brow. "And you don't think Shelby feels the same way about Trina? Or that Cody deserves the opportunity to say goodbye to his mother?"

Alex groaned and buried his face in his hands. "Okay, fine. Great. If Shelby and Cody are really going to return to Green Bay for the funeral, you have to help me dream up some plan that will keep them safe."

"That will be a challenge." Rafe scratched his jaw. "Maybe we need to come up with a different approach.

Maybe instead of avoiding the place, we should head there right away. Today."

"Are you crazy?" Alex nearly shouted. "No. Absolutely not. Risk Cody's life? And Shelby's?"

"Calm down and think this through logically," Rafe said in a stern voice. "Trina's shooting triggered a domino effect. Shelby and Cody were traced to Kayla's bed-and-breakfast. Then Bobby Drake's death. Now this stuff with Marilyn." He shook his head slowly. "Marilyn's disappearing act might be nothing, but I think we're missing putting pieces of this puzzle together because we're hiding out instead of being in the thick of things in Green Bay."

Alex clenched his jaw. Rafe was right. If not for Shelby and Cody being in danger, he wouldn't think twice about heading back to Green Bay. Except for one tiny problem. "Have you forgotten I'm not cleared to return to active duty?"

Rafe glanced down at his injured right arm. "How accurate are you with your left hand?"

"Not accurate enough," he responded tersely, opening and closing the fingers of his left hand, wishing for the impossible. "I can hit a large target from a distance of fifty feet without a problem, but anything requiring more finesse or a longer distance…" he shrugged. "I wouldn't bet anyone else's life on my ability, that's for sure."

Rafe pursed his lips thoughtfully. "If you can shoot from a distance of fifty feet, you can easily play bodyguard for Shelby and Cody once they're safely tucked inside a hotel. That gives me and Logan some time to dig under some rocks to see what we can uncover."

Exasperated, he stared at his partner. "That's it? That's your plan?"

Rafe scowled. "Do you have a better one?"

Alex closed his eyes and told himself to get a grip. No reason to take out his lousy mood on Rafe. It wasn't his partner's fault that the thought of Shelby and Cody being exposed to danger made him sweat. "No," he said finally. "I don't have a better one. But if anything happens to Shelby or Cody…" He couldn't finish the thought.

"You need to have a little faith, my friend," Rafe said quietly.

"I have faith in you," Alex protested.

"Not me. Faith in God. You need to reach out to the Lord, putting yourself in His hands."

His gaze caught on the cross Rafe wore around his neck and knew his partner was serious. Never in a million years would he have imagined having this conversation with Rafe. "Is that what you do?" he finally asked.

"Absolutely." Rafe leaned forward, his expression earnest. "And you can, too. Shelby would be more than happy to offer you guidance if needed."

He knew that much was true. And he suddenly felt sick at the possibility Rafe might be developing personal feelings for Shelby. After all, they shared the same beliefs.

"You like Shelby, don't you?" he asked.

"Of course I like her." For a minute Rafe looked puzzled and then suddenly he threw his head back and laughed. "Relax. I admire Shelby but I'm not interested in her on a personal level."

"Good." He couldn't deny the overwhelming sense of relief. As much as he knew he didn't deserve a woman like Shelby, he found he didn't want to imagine her with any other man, either.

Rafe's cell phone rang and he glanced at the screen. "Logan," he greeted the caller. "What's going on?"

Alex tensed, knowing Logan Quail wouldn't have called without a good reason. He watched Rafe expectantly, as his partner's face turned stone cold.

Shelby chose that moment to return. "Cody's getting bored."

"In a minute," Alex said, waiting for Rafe to finish. When his partner hung up the phone, he asked, "What's going on?"

Rafe glanced at Shelby and then back at Alex, letting out a heavy sigh. "Someone threw a firebomb at Shelby's car."

NINE

Shelby let out a shocked gasp. Alex stared at Rafe in horror. "Where was her car parked?" Was her house gone? Her day care center? He braced himself for the worst.

Rafe gave a curt nod as if he'd anticipated the question. "Not directly in front of her day care center, thankfully, but close enough to cause damage."

"Damage? What kind of damage?" Shelby swayed and Alex jumped up to lead her toward the nearest chair before she collapsed. "The children?" she asked in an agonized tone.

His chest squeezed painfully. Today was Monday, so Shelby's day care was likely full of kids.

"Logan is on the scene and he'll keep us updated," Rafe said, downplaying the topic of potential casualties. "The timing of the firebomb happened when most of the kids were outside in the backyard."

"But the infants don't go outside in the winter." Shelby's eyes filled with tears. "I'll never forgive myself if something happens to one of my children. Never."

Alex gently squeezed her hands trying to offer strength and support. "Shelby, this isn't your fault. No one will blame you."

What was going on? Why the sudden act of violence? At this late stage in the game, especially after Trina's death, it didn't make sense.

Unless there had been a tracking device on her car. And this was some sort of bizarre warning.

Shelby looked like she was in a daze repeating, "My children, my children," over and over again.

Helpless, Alex speared Rafe with a hard look. "Do you really think it's still a good idea for Shelby and Cody to go to the funeral?" he demanded.

"Alex," Rafe started, but he was quickly interrupted.

"Listen to me. Why would someone toss a firebomb at Shelby's car, huh? No rational reason other than as a dire warning to stay away. A warning we'd be idiots to ignore. The last place she and Cody should go is back to Green Bay."

"Maybe the firebomb was meant to destroy the tracking device? Or what if it *was* an effort to keep Shelby and Cody away? Because whoever threw it knew you'd react like this?" Rafe pointed out with infuriating logic. "And if that's the case, you'd be playing right into their hand by refusing to let them attend the funeral."

"I don't care." His gut clenched with the thought of anything happening to Shelby or Cody. "They're not going."

"Yes, we are." Shelby seemed to snap out of her trance to join the conversation. "Cody needs closure. Somehow, someway we need to find a way to take him."

He wanted to yank his hair out of his head in frustration. But he already knew from experience that yelling and arguing wasn't going to work. "Think about it, Shelby," he pleaded. "Please, think this through."

"I am trying to think it through," she said, looking suddenly exhausted. "I know we have to keep him safe, yet I also don't want Cody to have emotional issues for the rest of his life. Maybe it would be best to take Cody to see a child psychologist before making a final decision. I don't want him to be in danger. If the psychologist doesn't feel it's important for Cody to be there, to say goodbye to his mother, then I won't take him."

Rafe's phone rang again. "Logan? What's the status?" Rafe listened for a moment, and then his face relaxed. "No injuries," he repeated aloud for their benefit. "Thanks for letting us know."

Alex chest expanded with a wave of overwhelming relief.

Shelby closed her eyes and dropped her chin to her chest. "Thank You, Lord," she whispered.

Alex silently echoed the heartfelt prayer. If Rafe was right, someone had gone to great lengths to scare Shelby away.

Because of Cody?

Alex knew he couldn't hold off any longer.

"Shelby, it's time." At her blank look, he clarified. "I need to talk to Cody. We need to know what he saw."

Shelby wanted to protest, but she couldn't deny the truth. Her children at the day care center had been put at risk. Because of her. Because of the bad man Cody had seen.

As much as she didn't want Cody to relive those awful memories, she didn't seem to have much of an alternative.

"He'll be upset," she said in a low voice. "Remember how he reacted to seeing blood?"

"I know," Alex agreed softly. "I don't want to hurt him any more than you do. Let's think about it for a bit. There must be some way we can uncover his memories without causing too much harm."

"Art therapy is often used for troubled kids," Shelby said slowly. "I'm not an expert, but we learned a little about it in college."

"Worth a try." Alex turned to Rafe. "Can you find some art supplies?"

"Sure."

"Could we take Cody outside for a while?" Shelby asked. "He lost interest in the cartoons fairly quickly and I think the fresh air would do him good."

"I'll make another sweep of the area before I go to the store," Rafe offered.

"I'll go with you," Alex said. When he stood she caught a glimpse of a handgun tucked into the back waistband of his jeans, mostly hidden behind his denim shirt. "Give us a few minutes before you get Cody's coat and boots on, all right?"

She nodded, disturbed at the very real evidence of the danger. Was she being stubborn, insisting on going to Trina's funeral? Maybe. Yet she couldn't tolerate knowing that this was Cody's last chance to say goodbye to his mother. She wanted to do what was right for him.

Cody was thrilled with the chance to go outside to play in the snow. She waited for Alex to return before getting Cody dressed in his winter gear.

"Would you like to build a snowman?" she asked, pasting a bright smile on her face.

"Yeah!" Full of energy he dashed outside. She quickened her pace to keep up.

"Do you want to help?" she asked Alex, as he followed more slowly, alertly scanning the area.

"No, I'd rather watch."

She understood he meant keeping an eye out for anyone suspicious and turned her attention to Cody. The back part of the hotel had a large area of the parking lot no one had bothered to snowplow. Putting aside her worries, she threw herself into making this fun for Cody, showing him how to start the base of the snowman. The snow was wet and heavy, perfect for packing. Cody helped with more enthusiasm than skill.

When she and Cody struggled to get the second snowball placed on top of the first, Alex jumped in to help. She noticed Cody brightened the moment Alex began paying attention to him. He constantly looked to his father for approval.

Their snowman was a bit lopsided, but she didn't care. And neither did Cody.

"Our snowman needs a hat," Cody declared.

"Here, Cody, use mine." She was surprised when Alex stepped in to offer his own. And when Cody couldn't reach, Alex lifted him up so that Cody could place the hat on the snowman's head.

Watching father and son interact caused a lump to form in the back of her throat.

When she glanced back at Alex, she caught a hint of longing in his eyes. As if he'd regretted not joining them in building the snowman from the beginning. For a moment she saw a glimpse of what their life could be like, if both of them raised Cody together.

A true family.

The idea caught her off guard. Yet the more she

thought about it, the more she realized it really wasn't so surprising. She'd grown closer to Alex during these past few days than she'd ever been to any other man. And wouldn't it be wonderful for Cody to have two parents who loved him?

She told herself to get a grip. Alex didn't embrace her Christian lifestyle. She'd gotten the impression he might be open to the idea—he'd agreed to have Cody raised with Christian beliefs—but she couldn't share her life with someone who didn't share her faith.

She started toward him, but then Rafe returned with the art supplies, and the moment was gone.

"Good job." She applauded Cody when he found matching rocks for the snowman's eyes and a pinecone for the nose. She held him up so he could complete the snowman's face himself.

"Who's ready for lunch?" Rafe asked, as he hauled several sacks of food and art supplies from the SUV.

"I am!" Cody shouted, squirming out of her grip and running toward Rafe.

"We'll talk to him after lunch," Alex said softly.

She nodded, knowing she'd run out of time and excuses.

Watching the way Shelby played with Cody as they built a big, if lopsided, snowman, Alex realized she was a natural when it came to taking care of children.

Owning and operating a day care center was probably part of the reason, but everything Shelby did with Cody revealed the depth of her love for the boy.

She was Cody's surrogate mother, in every way. He admired everything about Shelby. The way she bravely faced her past. The way she helped Cody. The way she cared about the people in her life.

He found himself hoping she included him in her sphere of caring. Because his feelings for her were growing into something more intense than mere friendship.

Even though this wasn't the time or the place for anything more.

As they ate peanut butter and jelly sandwiches and apples for lunch, he couldn't get the image of her carefree laughing face out of his mind. For those brief moments outside, she'd seemed happy.

But not any more. The tiny brackets around her mouth told him that she was dreading the moment he began questioning Cody.

He wasn't feeling too great about it himself.

Typical Shelby, though, she didn't whine or complain, but got right to work as soon as she'd finished clearing away the lunch mess.

"Cody, look at what Mr. Rafe brought for you." She spread out the large sheets of paper on the small hotel table and opened up the container of crayons. She spilled them all over the table, so it would be easy to pick out whichever colors he preferred. "Would you like to draw pictures?"

"Yeah!" Cody knelt on one of the chairs, so he could reach the table. "Are you going to draw with me?"

"Of course." Shelby sat across from Cody, her expression thoughtful. "What should we draw?"

Alex stayed back with Rafe, allowing Shelby to take the lead. Obviously he didn't have the same experience she had with kids.

"How about a snowman?" Cody asked.

"No, we already made a snowman outside." Shelby pretended to think. "Maybe we should draw the marina?"

Even Alex could tell Cody had tensed up. "I dunno," he hedged.

Shelby leaned forward, brushing a hand over Cody's blond hair. "Cody, do you remember the night you saw the bad man?"

His green eyes widened until they seemed to take up his entire face. "Yes."

"Would you be able to draw a picture of the bad man for us?" she asked, gently. "Please? It's very important."

He stared down at the blank piece of paper in front of him, and Alex knew if Cody refused he wasn't going to force the issue. They'd simply have to figure out what happened some other way.

"Okay," he said, picking up the black crayon.

Alex held his breath as Cody began to draw. Shelby worked on her own picture, choosing to draw sailboats on the water, but kept her attention on what Cody was doing.

"What is that, a car?" she asked when Cody put down the black crayon.

He nodded. "I saw the bad man through my window."

Alex glanced at Shelby in surprise, but she was holding Cody's gaze. "You were in the backseat, here?" she asked, pointing to the picture.

"Yep. The bad man was yelling at my mom." For a moment his lower lip trembled and Alex had to stop himself from rushing over to stop Shelby's art therapy session.

"You're safe here with us now," Shelby said softly. "Your other dad and Mr. Rafe are here to keep you safe."

Cody glanced at Alex and Rafe, as if to reassure himself they were indeed there to keep him safe from harm.

"What did the bad man look like?" Shelby asked, pulling Cody's attention back to the picture. "Was he taller than your mom or shorter?"

"Tall. Really, really tall." Cody picked up the brown crayon and began drawing a man. He made a rectangular body, with stubby arms and legs sticking out of it. The figure was tall, much taller than the car.

"That's a great picture," Shelby said, admiring his work. "What color hair did the bad man have? Yellow like yours? Or dark like your dad's?"

Cody scrunched up his face. "I dunno. Mostly bald." He left the figure hairless and finished putting in the man's face, eyes, nose and mouth, and the mouth was frowning.

Then he picked up the red crayon and drew a wide red streak down the side of the man's head.

Alex sucked in a quick breath.

"Why is he bleeding?" Shelby asked in a calm tone.

"Mom hit him with a long skinny thing," Cody's voice was so quiet she could barely hear him. "He fell down and then she jumped in the car and drove away."

Alex closed his eyes, his stomach churning with guilt and regret. Cody should not have been forced to witness such violence. No wonder the poor kid had nightmares.

And it was all his fault. When Trina had offered to give inside information, he should have told her no. Should have encouraged her to stay far away from the shipyard.

Finding the mastermind behind the drug running operation shouldn't have cost Trina her life.

* * *

Shelby tried to keep calm, even though her stomach churned with nausea as she stared down at Cody's drawing.

"You're safe here with us," she reminded him, when he'd stopped working on his picture. "What else is in the picture? What was next to your car?"

Cody scrunched up his face for a moment, then picked up a navy blue crayon. "Big ships," he said, drawing a large rectangle to one side of the picture.

"Like in the shipyard?" Shelby asked, as she worked on her own drawing. She found herself drawing the marina, the morning the gunman had found Trina. Was the man with the gun the same person Cody had drawn with the blood streak on his face? It seemed likely, but she wasn't sure.

He nodded but didn't say anything, simply drawing more ships.

When Cody finished his picture, he shoved it away. Since he seemed to lose interest in the paper and crayons, she decided not to push. He'd opened himself up enough, she didn't want to add to his distress.

"There's a Disney movie on the television," Alex offered in a low voice. "Maybe he'd like to watch?"

"Sure." She knew they wanted to have Cody preoccupied while they discussed the details they'd uncovered. She took Cody into the connecting room and found the movie. He'd burned off enough energy building a snowman outside, that she thought he might fall asleep while watching.

"Mostly bald," Alex repeated as she walked back to

talk with the two men. "That should help us narrow our list of suspects."

She sat down with a sigh. "Maybe, but to Cody's mind, mostly bald could be short hair, like a military cut, too."

Alex grimaced. "And really, really tall doesn't mean much either, other than that the guy was taller than Trina."

"Let's re-create that night," Rafe suggested, looking at both Shelby's and Cody's pictures. "Cody drew large ships, as if he was in a car parked at the shipyard."

Alex leaned forward eagerly. "Cody is in the backseat of a car, while Trina goes to meet someone. Something happens and she's forced to defend herself, maybe with a baseball bat or a tire iron, hitting the bad guy. He goes down and she jumps into the car to escape. But she doesn't go back to her place because she thinks she'll be followed."

Shelby joined in the theorizing. "And she doesn't come to my place for the same reason. She calls me and insists I meet her at the marina because Cody's in danger. I drive down there and she's standing in the shadows of our father's yacht, the *Juliet*."

"How does the gunman know she's there?" Alex asked, when Shelby paused. "Does he have a tracking device on her? Or does he know her well enough to know she wouldn't go home or to Shelby's place?"

"Trina said something interesting when I met her down at the marina," Shelby said slowly. "She told me she'd made a terrible mistake. And that I needed to call you, Alex. No one else, not the police, not anyone but you." She stared for a moment at Cody's drawing. "So what was her mistake? Trusting the wrong person? Stephan?"

Alex exchanged a concerned look with Rafe. "Stephan isn't mostly bald," Alex pointed out. "And I would think if Cody had seen his stepfather, he would have said something to that effect, rather than calling him the bad man."

"Okay, that makes sense." Shelby nodded with relief. "But then who did Trina trust that turned out to be a terrible mistake?"

"Your father?" Alex said. "He's tall and mostly bald."

She narrowed her eyes. "Same argument as with Stephan. Cody knows his grandfather. He wouldn't have referred to him as the bad man, either."

"Maybe you're both wrong on that," Rafe spoke up. "Maybe the guy Trina was fighting with was wearing some sort of face mask obscuring his features?"

"No, I'm sure Cody would have said something about a mask." Shelby looked down at the drawing again, trying to imagine what Cody might have seen. "If they were arguing at an angle, or if the man's back was to Cody, it's possible he didn't get a good look at the man's face at all."

"He drew a frown," Rafe said tapping the guy's face on Cody's picture.

"The frown could be something he added because he heard them yelling." Shelby grimaced. "That might be simply the way he portrayed the man's anger onto the drawing."

Alex let out a heavy sigh. "So you're telling us Cody's description is basically useless? That we can't really narrow down any of the suspects unless they happen to be the same height or shorter than your sister or have a head full of hair?"

As much as she hated to admit it, she couldn't lie. "I think if it was dark, and Cody didn't get a good look at his face, then no, we can't narrow down any of the suspects. Stephan has always worn his hair long, and he's only a couple of inches taller than Trina, so we can probably take him off the list."

"But not Bobby Drake. Bobby was six feet tall and wore his hair in a crew cut," Rafe said.

Alex captured her gaze with his. "And not your father."

TEN

The minute the words left his mouth, Alex wanted to call them back. Especially when Shelby paled, bit her lip and looked away, a hint of angry desperation in her eyes.

What was wrong with him? Why couldn't he keep his big mouth shut? There was no reason to blurt out his true feelings like that.

Of course Trina and Shelby wanted to believe their father was innocent. Yet no matter how much she and Trina had protested, he just couldn't quite believe their father was innocent. His background research had shown how Jacobson had taken the shipping business from a struggling operation to amazing success within the first five years he'd owned the place. There was no denying Jacobson clearly possessed a keen mind for business. And that was exactly why Alex simply couldn't believe Russ Jacobson didn't know about the drugs coming in on his ships. A man that involved in his company had to know what was going on.

There was a long moment of silence while Rafe shifted uncomfortably in his seat.

"We have a long list of suspects," Rafe said finally.

"And I'm sure there are plenty of other people we haven't even considered."

"Trina seemed wary of involving the local authorities, Shelby commented in a low voice. "She specifically told me not to trust anyone, even the police."

"Exactly my point. There could be someone working on the inside," Rafe agreed. "There were many cops who had made it quite clear they didn't like the DEA homing in on their turf."

Shelby lifted her chin and regarded him steadily. "I think Rafe is right. We can't do anything from here. We need to be closer to the action. We need to head into Green Bay, the sooner the better."

Alex clenched his jaw, biting back a protest. Because she was right. Not that he had any intention of exposing Shelby or Cody to danger. No way was he going to allow them anywhere close to the so-called action. But he and Rafe needed to be closer to the scene. And besides, if she was really going to take Cody to Trina's funeral, then they'd need to figure out where the funeral home was located and how they were going to cover the various entrances and exits to keep everyone safe.

The idea of allowing Shelby and Cody out of his sight even for a second made him sweat. He wasn't going to let it happen unless he was absolutely certain they'd be protected.

"Logan is picking me up in an hour," Rafe announced. "Why don't you let us go into the city first? That way we can find a place for you to stay that's relatively close to where Trina's funeral will be."

Alex jumped on the opportunity to put off heading into Green Bay one moment earlier than they needed to.

"Sounds like an excellent plan. I'll call you in the morning before we leave."

"Wait a minute," Shelby protested. "Do we really need to wait until tomorrow? I want Cody to see a child psychologist as soon as possible. I'd like a professional opinion on whether or not he should attend his mother's funeral. And to do that, we need to get to Green Bay, sooner rather than later."

Alex raised his eyebrows in surprise. Still, maybe she was right. There was a good possibility the child psychologist would tell Shelby the funeral wasn't a good idea.

At least he could hope.

He quickly amended their plans. "It's better if we go in the morning, but I promise we'll get to Green Bay early enough so you can take Cody in to see someone."

Her expression mirrored her relief. "Thank you."

Cody chose that moment to join them, rubbing his eyes sleepily.

"I'm hungry," he announced.

"I'm sure you are, partner." Shelby glanced at him. "Normally he gets a snack in the afternoon to hold him over until dinnertime."

"Logan's pulling up to the hotel now," Rafe said when his cell phone went off. "I asked him to bring some things for Cody. Clothes and snacks."

"Wonderful," Shelby said warmly. "Thanks, Rafe."

"You're welcome, *amiga*." Rafe flashed a bright smile. "Why don't you and Cody come out to meet Logan?"

"Okay." Shelby quickly gathered their coats and bundled up Cody before following Rafe outside.

Alex stood near the window, watching them. Cody scooped up some snow and threw a snowball at Rafe.

There wasn't much power in the attempt, but Shelby laughed and Alex's gut tightened with awareness.

They didn't seem to be in any hurry to come back inside.

He couldn't deny he was out of his element when it came to being a father figure to Cody. He'd never spent much time around kids, until his most recent injury. His niece, Brianna, was a cutie and he'd enjoyed spending time with her over the past few months, but he didn't know the first thing about raising a child. Much less how his sister managed to do it on her own in the two years since her husband had died.

Shelby was a lot like Kayla. She would do just fine raising Cody on her own, too.

Wait a minute. He thrust his hands through his hair and spun away from the window. Was he seriously considering giving up custody of his son to Shelby?

The very thought tightened the knots in his stomach. He wasn't sure he knew how to be a good father, but the thought of giving Cody up didn't sit well, either. Yet shouldn't he worry about what was best for his son? Cody obviously considered Shelby to be his surrogate mother. And sadly, he was young enough that in a few years, his memories of Trina would likely fade away. Shelby would soon be the most important person in his life.

But didn't a boy need a father, too?

Maybe, but Shelby was a wonderful woman. It was very likely she'd meet a man one day. Someone like Rafe, who would be a great father to Cody.

A far better father than he could ever be.

Every cell of his being rejected the idea of Shelby finding someone else. But if he proved that her father was guilty, she wasn't going to forgive him anytime soon. And if that was the case, he knew he would give up custody of his son to Shelby.

He pulled his scattered thoughts together, when the group came back in, filling the small motel room.

"Logan," he greeted the tall, brown-haired agent who'd been sent to replace him. Logan Quail wore cowboy boots and a Stetson cowboy hat, but his voice only held the barest hint of his Southern roots.

"McCade. How's the arm?"

Alex shrugged, opening and closing the fingers of his damaged right hand. "It's still attached, I guess. I've been working on shooting left-handed."

If Logan was concerned about Alex's ability to get back into the field, he didn't show it. "Good. Things are heating up, big time. I think the case is about to be blown wide open."

A surge of adrenaline flowed through his veins. Along with a healthy dose of wariness. "I'd love to put this case to rest, but it would help to know where the source of the danger is coming from."

"Don't I know it," Logan agreed. He glanced at Shelby, who stood near Rafe. "How well do you know your stepmother?" he asked.

Shelby frowned. "Marilyn? Not very well. She's not my favorite person. Trina and I always believed she married my dad for his money."

Logan and Alex exchanged a look. "What makes you say that?"

Shelby shrugged. "She doesn't have just one materialistic bone in her body, she has several. From the moment she married my father, she has spent his money as if it washed up on the lakeshore along with the dead fish. Why all this interest in Marilyn?"

Logan threw a questioning glance at Alex, and he gave a subtle nod, indicating Logan could speak freely around Shelby.

"I did a little digging on Marilyn Hayes Jacobson," Logan said slowly. "She died about six years ago."

Shelby's jaw dropped. "What do you mean, she died?"

Logan's expression was grim. "A woman by the name of Marilyn Hayes with your stepmother's social security number has been dead for the past six years."

Alex narrowed his gaze. "So whoever this woman really is, she re-created herself six years ago? That's about the time we began hearing about the potential drug smuggling operation coming through Green Bay."

"I know." Logan looked at Shelby, who sank into a nearby chair as if her knees had gone weak. Shelby was strong, but Alex wondered just how many more shocks she could take before crumbling. "I'm sorry to dump this on you so abruptly, but I figured you needed to know, especially considering your father's company is knee deep in this mess. We're still trying to figure out exactly who Marilyn really is, but the fact that she's using a fake name and social security number is enough to put her at the top of our suspect list."

Alex couldn't deny the timing was right. And considering how Shelby and Trina weren't close to their stepmother, she wouldn't hesitate to eliminate one of them if they got in her way.

"So if Marilyn is at the top of the suspect list," he mused aloud, "that means Cody's bad man is likely working either for her or with her as a partner in crime."

* * *

Shelby's mind reeled at the news regarding her step-mother. Or maybe her soon to be ex-stepmother, if Marilyn had really moved out of her father's house.

Once Alex and Logan left, her room had seemed far too quiet. She stayed with Cody, until Alex poked his head through the connecting doorway and asked if she wanted to go down to eat in the diner.

"Yes, getting out of the hotel room for a while would be wonderful."

The diner wasn't very crowded, so they pretty much had the place to themselves. Once Cody had finished his chicken strips, he went over to the race car driver video game in the corner. He sat in the seat, clutching the steering wheel, making *vroom, vroom,* noises.

Alex stood and crossed over to put a few coins into the slot. "Push this button, here," he directed. "This starts the game. Now you can really drive the race car."

She couldn't help but smile when Cody shouted with glee as he maneuvered the video game. Alex came back to take the seat across from her. "He's having fun."

"I know. Thanks." She toyed with her water glass. "Alex, you said you wouldn't mind if we raised Cody as a Christian, right?"

He slowly nodded. "Yes, that's right."

"But yet, you're not a believer." It wasn't a question.

He hesitated. "You're right, I wasn't raised to be a believer. But I have to admit, that first night when Cody prayed for me, I was surprised and humbled to be included in his prayers. And then when we had to walk through the storm to find shelter, I prayed for the first time in my life."

She sucked in a surprised breath, her heart filling

with joyful hope. "Really? Then God answered both of our prayers, guiding us to shelter."

Alex's smile was crooked. "I have to agree, since I couldn't see much of anything with the snow and the wind in my face and yet managed to find exactly what we needed."

She was so happy to hear Alex wanted to have faith. "I'd love for you to join my church. We can do bible studies and meet so many great people." The possibilities were endless.

Alex's smile faded. "Maybe," he said cautiously. "But if I am able to go back to work, I won't be around much."

Her hope collapsed like a deflated balloon. "What do you mean? You're Cody's father. Of course you have to be around for him."

He sighed. "Shelby, my work with the DEA is important to me. My best friend in high school died of a drug overdose. I've dedicated my life to keeping drugs off the streets. If my aim with my left arm becomes good enough that I can stay in the field, I will."

"And what about Cody?"

He dropped his gaze. "I'll grant you sole custody of Cody."

She stared at him, hardly able to believe what she was hearing. Surely she must have misunderstood. "You'd give him up completely?"

"Yes, I would. If that's what was best for him."

That night, Shelby couldn't fall asleep. Alex wasn't the man she'd thought him to be, if he could actually consider giving up his son.

Certainly being a DEA agent was admirable. And his

reasons for dedicating his life to eradicating drugs from the streets were honorable, too. To lose someone you cared about to drugs was horrible. But surely there were other ways to help his cause? A path that didn't push him toward giving up custody of his son.

She closed her eyes on a wave of regret. Her dream of becoming a family with Cody and Alex was nothing more than foolish fantasy.

But this wasn't about her. It was about Cody. And Alex. Even without the family she'd always wanted, they needed each other.

Lifting her heart and her mind to God, she prayed. *Dear Lord, help me understand Your will. I love Cody so much and I've begun to care for Alex, too. Guide me toward Your path, Amen.*

When her troubled soul was soothed by prayer, she drifted off to sleep hoping Alex was praying for guidance, too.

The next morning, Alex agreed to drive into Green Bay. She was relieved to know Cody would soon get the help he needed, but she couldn't deny a flicker of fear.

Trina had been murdered only three days ago. And since that time, someone had not only followed them, but had tried to kill them. She wasn't sure what awaited them in Green Bay.

Heavenly Father, keep us safe in Your care.

When they'd finished breakfast in the diner, they packed up Kayla's SUV and headed into Green Bay.

"You're awfully quiet this morning," Alex said, casting a glance in her direction.

She tried to smile. "I've been thinking a lot about what you said last night."

He gave a slight frown. "I thought you'd be happy to know you'll have custody."

"I love Cody and would gladly take custody of him. But I also believe a child should have two actively involved parents." She paused before asking, "What if you can't go back to the DEA? What then?"

Alex didn't answer for a long moment, his gaze glued to the road. The sun was shining brightly and the temperature had warmed up enough that much of the snow from the storm was already melting. "I don't know."

His response wasn't reassuring. "But you would stay part of Cody's life?" she persisted.

"I'd try," he finally answered.

"Praying for guidance may help," she said slowly. "I'm certain God would show you the right path to take, much like He did during the snowstorm."

He shot a surprised glance in her direction, as if the thought had never occurred to him. After several long seconds, he gave a slow nod. "Maybe I will."

Satisfied that she'd done the best she could, Shelby turned her attention to Cody. Earlier that morning she'd used the hotel phone to call Debbi, her day care center assistant, to find out the extent of the damage from the firebomb. Debbi had confirmed they would have to be closed for a few days until the front window glass was replaced. So far, only one parent had taken their child out of the program. Shelby could only hope it wasn't the first of many.

Debbi had also given her the name of her brother-in-law, Dr. Kade Zander who happened to be a child psychologist.

"He's generally pretty booked," Debbi had told her,

"but as a favor to me, Kade said he'd make room for Cody whenever you need him to come in."

Shelby had been thrilled and had requested Kade's phone number. When she'd talked to him, he'd agreed to see Cody at noon that day, over his lunch hour. Shelby had been grateful for the favor. She really wanted a professional's opinion on what was best for Cody.

After a few hours of driving, Alex pulled up to a large, well-known hotel, located not far from the church where Trina's funeral services were to be held.

"I hope you're not upset, but I reserved a two-bedroom suite for us," he said. "There's a living room and small kitchen area in the center and I thought it would be good for Cody. And then the two bedrooms are on opposite ends of the suite."

She was glad he'd thought about Cody's needs and her privacy. "A suite should be fine, if we can afford it."

He gave her an odd look. "We can afford it. Logan booked the room under his name, so we don't have to worry about anyone finding us here."

She hoped he was right. The room wasn't ready yet, so Alex drove them to Dr. Zander's office.

"I'll pick you up in an hour," he said. "In the meantime I'm meeting with Rafe and Logan. We'll pick up some groceries after lunch."

"All right." She took Cody's hand as they went inside. The waiting area was full of toys and he didn't need any urging to find something to play with.

Dr. Kade Zander met with her for a few minutes first, and she immediately liked the gentle, soft-spoken doctor. She'd explained what Cody had been through and her dilemma about taking him to the funeral, especially her fears related to his mental health balanced against the need to keep him safe.

"Closure is very important for young children," he admitted. "My first instinct is to agree he should go, if you think it's safe enough. Let me meet with him first, to see how traumatized he's been."

"I understand," she agreed. Would the funeral be safe? She found it hard to imagine that someone would try to harm Cody in the middle of a public funeral. Surely there were precautions they could take.

Dr. Zander took Cody back into another playroom, and Shelby settled in to wait. She leafed through various parenting magazines, even though she was dying to know what was going on in the other room.

The forty-five minutes seemed to drag by slowly, but when Cody came back out, he appeared to be his usual happy self. The doctor gestured for her to come over.

"Cody is adjusting fairly well, but I do think going to the funeral will be good for him," he told her. "He misses his mother, but I get the sense she wasn't always the most dominant person in his life. He talks about you a lot."

She couldn't help but smile. "I spend a lot of time with him. Between the hours he's at the day care center and the times he spends at my apartment, we've become very close."

Dr. Zander nodded. "It's apparent he loves you very much. Death is a difficult concept for children to understand. Telling him that his mother is in heaven certainly helps, but he sometimes makes comments about his mother coming back, so I do believe attending the funeral will give some closure, if precautions can be taken to make sure he's safe. I'd be happy to see him on a weekly or biweekly basis if you think it would help going forward."

"I would like that," Shelby confessed. "I've been so worried I'm making things worse for him, rather than better."

"You're doing fine," he reassured. "Considering everything that has happened, I think Cody's doing remarkably well."

"Thank you." Relieved she'd been on the right track, she offered her hand. "I feel much better now."

"My opinion is only based on my expertise regarding a child's emotional health," he warned gently. "It's your decision if the potential physical danger is worth the risk."

She nodded, her relief fading. "I know."

He seemed satisfied with that. "I've been recommending your day care center to my clients," Dr. Zander said, clasping her hand gently yet firmly. "I believe faith is very important in raising children."

"Debbi and I certainly appreciate it." She couldn't help thinking about the damage from the firebomb. It wasn't her fault, but the end result was the same. She couldn't blame parents for taking their children out of her center to attend someplace else. "Thanks again."

Alex was waiting outside when they left the office building. "Are you hungry?" he asked. "I don't want to go anywhere public, but we could pick up something at a fast food place to take back to the hotel."

"Sounds good."

Alex pulled into a parking lot of a restaurant offering buckets of fried chicken. Shelby volunteered to stay in the car with Cody. Directly across the street was a small pub, and when a familiar woman stepped outside, glancing around furtively before rushing over to her car, Shelby sucked in a harsh breath.

"Marilyn!" She couldn't take her eyes off her step-mother. Marilyn seemed to be in a big hurry, and somewhat upset, her eyes red and swollen when she jumped into her car and quickly drove away.

Had Marilyn been inside, meeting someone? A man? Cody's bad man?

Alex opened the door and handed her the food. She took it, but when he slid in beside her, she grabbed his arm. "Alex, I just saw Marilyn. She left that pub across the street, looking upset. What if she was meeting someone?"

He glanced in the direction she indicated. "I don't believe it. Look who's coming out now."

She glanced over and saw a tall man walk out into the sunlight. In a heartbeat, she recognized him. "Mayor Flynn."

"Yeah. He's tall and mostly bald, just like Cody's bad man."

ELEVEN

A sense of excitement hummed in Alex's bloodstream, like it always did when he was on the verge of breaking open a case. This was the part of his job he liked, bringing the bad guys to justice. He stared at the mayor, watching as the guy walked towards a shiny black Lexus.

"Do you think Marilyn was meeting the mayor?" Shelby's voice sounded incredulous. "That she's cheating on my father with him?"

"That's one explanation," he murmured with a frown. "But you mentioned she looked upset, so we shouldn't be hasty, jumping to conclusions." He turned on the SUV engine and pulled out of the parking lot, heading in the opposite direction.

"But he can't be—" she stopped and glanced back at Cody and Alex knew she didn't want to say too much in front of the boy.

He didn't respond, his mind whirling with possibilities. They knew Marilyn wasn't who she said she was, but for Mayor Flynn to be Cody's bad man seemed a bit of a stretch. As Mayor, James Flynn's life was very much in the public eye. Yet at the same time, he could use his power to influence the local police investigation.

Like telling everyone Trina's murder was likely a robbery gone bad. And pushing for a quick closure on the case.

Still, to be fair, Cody's description covered a wide range of people. Too many to be of much help, really.

"Isn't City Hall on the other end of town?" Shelby asked, her brow puckered in a tiny frown.

"Yeah. If they were having an affair, it's possible they'd traveled all the way over here to minimize their chances of being seen."

"If I hadn't insisted on bringing Cody to Dr. Zander, we wouldn't have seen them," she said in a quiet tone.

He couldn't deny the truth of her words. In the rearview mirror he could see Cody sitting in the backseat. "Did Cody see him?" he asked, lowering his voice too, so Cody wouldn't hear.

"I don't think so," Shelby said with a grimace. "And I didn't think to point him out."

"There's no guarantee he'd have recognized him, anyway," Alex assured her. "And we could show him a picture. The mayor's photo would be easy to find on the Internet."

"Which may not help, since we don't know if Cody got a good look at his face," she reminded him.

"I know." He returned to the hotel as quickly as possible, knowing he needed to get in touch with Rafe and Logan about the latest turn in events.

"Dr. Zander believes Cody can benefit from attending Trina's funeral," Shelby said, breaking the silence. "If you think it's safe enough to go."

He glanced over at her. "Really? And if I don't think it's safe enough?"

For a moment, she looked uncertain. "If you say it isn't safe, we won't go. I trust your judgment. But Alex. I really want to attend, especially if going will help Cody deal with the loss of his mother. His emotional health is important, too. The funeral is going to be crowded with lots of people attending." The all-too familiar stubborn glint was in her eyes. "This is really important. Can you look me in the eye and tell me there's absolutely no way you, Rafe and Logan can't ensure Cody's safety?"

Alex let out a deep, heavy sigh. He couldn't look her in the eye and say that, because she was right. The crowded funeral wasn't exactly the time he would choose to take out a young witness. Yet on the other hand, the thought of his son being in danger, no matter how remote, made him cautious. His earlier enthusiasm for the case evaporated, leaving a vague, nauseous feeling in its place.

"We'll see what we can do," Alex reluctantly promised.

When they finished their lunch, Shelby took Cody into their bedroom. She didn't close the door and Alex could hear her asking if Cody wanted to watch a movie or read some of his picture books.

He called his partner, updating Rafe and Logan on the newest development with Mayor Flynn and Marilyn, along with Shelby's plan to attend Trina's funeral.

When he finished with his phone calls, he stayed on the sofa, eavesdropping on Shelby's conversation with Cody.

"I know my mom is in heaven, but why can't we visit her?" Cody asked.

"Heaven is where God lives, Cody. People on earth

like you and me can't go up to visit. When we die, our souls go up to live with God in heaven. And that's where your mom's soul is right now."

"So she can't come down to visit me, either?" Cody asked.

"No, sweetheart, I'm afraid not. But you can still talk to your mom, just like you talk to God when you pray."

"Is she going to be lonely up there, all by herself?" Cody asked.

"Oh, no, Cody, she won't be by herself. Heaven is a wonderful, beautiful, peaceful place with lots of people your mom knew and loved when they lived on earth. Once souls get up in heaven, they don't want to come back."

Alex smiled a bit at the thought of Trina being in heaven. Listening to Cody and Shelby's conversation about God and heaven made him remember the night he'd waded through the snowstorm, carrying Cody and leading Shelby with a rope, praying for the first time that he could remember.

Shelby thought God had answered their prayers and looking back, he could only agree. There was certainly no other logical explanation as to how he'd managed to find the shelter of those far trees. He couldn't see but scant inches in front of his face. One minute he was walking blindly, wondering how much longer Shelby would be able to keep up and the next, he'd stumbled onto the shelter.

Some people might argue luck, but at that moment, he'd known that he hadn't found the shelter of those trees on his own. He'd had help.

Guidance from God.

Shelby had suggested he seek help in figuring out his

future through prayer, but somehow he didn't think it would work the same way. Just because God had answered one prayer, did that mean He would answer more? Feeling a little foolish, he closed his eyes and opened his heart.

I'm new at this stuff, Lord, but I need Your help to know what I should do with my life. Since Toby's death, I've vowed to do my best to keep drugs off the streets. But being a DEA agent isn't the best career for a man raising a son. Shelby will be a good mother for Cody, of that I have no doubt. But I'm not sure how to be an equally good father. I need direction, Lord. Show me the way.

He opened his eyes and glanced around. Okay, it was silly to think that God would simply drop some sort of note out of the sky telling him what to do with the rest of his life. But deep down, there was a strange sense of peace.

Shelby came out of the bedroom, half-closing the door behind her.

"Is he sleeping?"

She smiled and nodded. "Yes. Fell asleep while I was telling him my favorite Bible story."

"I don't know any Bible stories," he confessed. "But I did what you suggested. I prayed for guidance as to what I should do with my career and my future."

Her expression brightened and he was amazed at how beautiful she was. "I'm glad. I just know God will help you decide what's best."

He gestured for Shelby to take a seat beside him. "Is it really that easy?" he asked. "To become a believer?"

She laughed, a light musical sound that warmed his

heart. "Yes, it's really that easy. Having faith and praying are a big part of what is important."

"I'd like to learn more," Alex admitted slowly.

Shelby reached over to take his hand in hers, curling her slight fingers around his. He caught his breath at her soft caress. "I'd love to help you in any way I can," she murmured.

The way she stared at him, so intently, made him feel short of breath, as if there wasn't enough oxygen in the room. Holding her hand like this, as if they were the only two people in the world at this moment, gave him the insane urge to draw her close, enveloping her in a tight embrace.

And the way she was looking at him, shyly curious, made him wonder how she'd respond to his touch.

Considering her past experience with men, he knew he had to go slowly, lest he frighten her. She'd allowed him to help warm her up while they were in the shelter of the snowstorm, but at that moment, their embrace hadn't been personal.

"Shelby," he whispered, reaching up to brush a stray curl off her cheek. Her skin was satiny smooth and he was amazed to see his fingers were trembling. He wanted to tell her how special she was but didn't know how. Gently, he cupped her cheek with his hand, brushing the silky softness with the pad of his thumb.

Her eyes widened at the caress. But she didn't pull away. Just the opposite. She tilted her head, leaning into his palm.

His breath strangled in his throat and he captured her gaze with his, lowering his head, slowly, so as not to scare her, wanting nothing more than to steal a kiss.

His cell phone rang. No doubt Rafe or Logan with news on the Mayor Flynn angle. He froze, torn by duty and desire.

Duty won. Regretfully he dropped his hand from Shelby's face and turned away, reaching for his cell phone.

Wishing he'd met Shelby at another time or place.

The skin of her cheek still tingled long after Alex's hand had dropped away. She sat on the sofa, unable to move, her emotions in turmoil as Alex spoke to Rafe.

He'd been about to kiss her. She'd known it the moment he'd looked deep into her eyes. And even more shocking, at least to her, was that she'd wanted him to.

She licked suddenly dry lips and tried to understand what was happening to her. She avoided men, had resigned herself to living her life alone, without male companionship. Yet with Alex, she couldn't remain indifferent.

She cared about him. More than she ought to. Because while she knew she could trust him, while she firmly believed Alex would never physically hurt her, she wasn't so sure she could trust him with her heart.

"Stephan Kirkland called Shelby?" Alex interrupted her thoughts when he swung around to face her. It took her a moment to realize he and Rafe were discussing her. There was another pause as Alex listened to what Rafe was saying. "I don't like it, Rafe," Alex said with a scowl. "I don't want her anywhere near the guy."

She frowned at his commanding tone. She knew Alex wanted to keep her safe, but he couldn't shut her off from the rest of the world forever. And besides, Stephan might not be Cody's father, but he'd still raised the boy for the past four years. He had a right to know what was going on. And she knew it would be safe to see him— he was too short to be Cody's bad man. "I'd like to meet with him."

Alex's gaze drilled a hole into her for a long moment, before he swung away. "I need time to think about it," he said in an abrupt tone. "I'll get back to you." Clearly irritated, he snapped his phone shut.

"Did Stephan say why he wants to meet with me?" she asked, when he didn't offer any further information.

"He claims he wants to talk to you about releasing custody rights to Cody." Alex's scowl deepened as he continued to pace the center of the room. "But I'm not buying his story. I don't trust him."

The vehemence in his tone surprised her. "I thought we basically ruled Stephan out as Cody's bad guy?"

"No one is ruled out," Alex responded flatly. "If Stephan was safe, why didn't Trina send you to him?"

He had a point. She remembered specifically asking Trina about Stephan and if he could help. "Well, she also told me not to trust anyone, even the police, so apparently she didn't want me to take Cody to anyone but you. That doesn't mean Stephan is guilty."

Alex spun around to face her. "Can you repeat exactly what she said?"

It was three days ago, but Trina's words were indelibly imprinted on her brain. "She told me she had made a terrible mistake and asked if I'd take Cody and keep him safe. She told me to call you, because you were Cody's real father and once you knew about him, you'd keep him safe. I asked her if Stephan knew, and she nodded and told me she had never listed Stephan as the father on Cody's birth certificate. She said, 'He can't help,' meaning Stephan. Then she told me not to trust anyone, especially the police."

"Especially the police?" He stared down at his cell phone for a moment, as if it were some sort of foreign object. "If the mayor is involved, he could easily have a cop on the inside working for him," he murmured. "And someone inside the police force would have the ability to trace Trina's cell phone to Kayla's bed-and-breakfast."

"It's all my fault," she whispered.

He shook his head. "No, it's mine. I should have realized the possibility earlier. Especially after hearing from Rafe that Holden didn't have any suspects or a clear motive for murder, and that he was getting pressure to close the case quickly."

"No clear motive?" Had everyone gone crazy? "What about giving inside information to the DEA? Surely that's motive."

Alex glanced away. "We haven't said anything about that. Right now, it's better for us if the police do conclude robbery. Once we know who's behind the drug smuggling, then we can gather the evidence needed to pin Trina's murder on them."

Troubled, she dropped her argument. Because what he said made some sense. If there was a dirty cop inside the police force, they would want Trina's murder covered up too, so pushing for a more thorough investigation wasn't going to help.

She rubbed the aching area on the side of her temple. "So we can't trust the police. I get that part. But Stephan wouldn't hurt Cody. And Cody would have recognized him if Stephan had been the one arguing with Trina. So there's really no reason I couldn't meet with him."

Alex clenched his jaw. "I don't like it."

She tried to hide her uneasiness. "He might know something, Alex. He was married to Trina, after all. Granted, they were having marital troubles, but for all we know, Trina's mistake involved trusting the police, not anything specifically about Stephan."

"I still don't like it," he muttered. But the resigned expression in his eyes convinced her that he'd already given in. "You're not going alone. I'll be with you and we're going to meet with him in a very public place."

"You?" Once again, she was surprised. "Won't going out in public risk your cover?"

A grim smile tugged at his mouth. "If you'd seen me as a longshoreman, you'd know how different I look now. I grew my hair long and dyed it dishwater blond. With a scruffy beard and dark brown contact lenses, even Rafe had trouble recognizing me. Besides, my cover is the least of our worries. The fact that I was jumped and stabbed three months ago indicates my cover has already been blown."

Understanding hit hard. "You're in danger, Alex. They wanted to kill you, too."

He didn't disagree. "I'll call Rafe so he and Logan can help prepare for this meeting with Stephan. Unless you've changed your mind?"

"No. I haven't changed my mind."

Shelby could tell Alex wasn't happy, even though he hid his feelings behind a brisk no-nonsense attitude. He and Logan had picked a busy restaurant as the place for Shelby to meet Stephan. Logan was seated not far from their table while Rafe had stayed back at the hotel with Cody.

She and Alex were already seated in a booth when Stephan arrived. Trina's husband looked awful, as if he hadn't gotten any sleep since Trina's murder.

"Thanks for meeting me," Stephan said, sliding into the empty space across from them. Shelby was pinned in the corner of the booth, between Alex's large frame and the wall of the restaurant. He glanced nervously at Alex. "Who's your friend?"

"I'm with the federal government and Shelby's in our protection," Alex told him. "That's all you need to know."

Stephan didn't seem too surprised to see a federal agent sitting beside Shelby. He ignored Alex and turned his attention to her. "How's Cody?"

"He's doing as well as can be expected," Shelby answered.

Stephan nodded grimly. "I wanted to know what your plans were. I know he's not my son, but I need to make sure someone is going to take formal custody of him."

"Have you always known he wasn't your son?" Shelby asked.

Stephan slowly nodded. "Yeah. I was upset at first, but I loved Trina. And we'd both made mistakes that were better left in the past."

"You didn't offer to adopt him?" Alex asked.

"No. Trina didn't suggest it, so I didn't offer." Guilt flashed in Stephan's gaze and she realized now why Trina had been happy to let Cody stay overnight with her so many times. Stephan was bothered by Cody's presence. "He's not a bad kid," Stephan continued, "but I didn't want to be responsible for someone else's son."

Shelby could feel Alex tense up beside her, and she hastened to interject. "I'm going to request custody of Cody."

Stephan looked relieved. "Good. I'm glad to hear that. It's always been obvious to me how much you love him."

"When was the last time you saw Trina?" Alex asked, changing the subject.

Stephan sighed and scrubbed his hand over his face, clearly exhausted. "The police have already taken my statement, why don't you ask them?"

"Because I'm asking you." Alex's voice reminded her of steel wrapped in velvet. "Did you know about the drugs coming in on Jacobson ships?"

Stephan didn't look surprised. "Yeah, I suspected there was something going on and stumbled upon the truth. I brought it up with Trina and she told me under-cover agents were working on it, so I should keep my mouth shut."

Shelby saw the flash of anger in his eyes. "Is that why you moved out?"

Stephan flushed guiltily and averted his gaze. "Yeah. I mean, I didn't like the ways things were going. Trina was different, acting weird and frankly, I didn't want to be dragged into danger."

"Did Russ Jacobson know about the drugs?" Alex persisted.

Stephan shrugged. "I didn't say anything to him, but I don't know how he couldn't. He knows everything that goes on in the shipyard."

Shelby couldn't believe Stephan had known about

the drugs coming in on her father's ships. Seemed like everyone had known but her. Yet no matter what, she still couldn't believe her father was guilty. There had to be some logical explanation. "When was the last time you saw Trina?" she asked.

"The night before she died." Stephan's expression was haggard. "I kept my mouth shut about the drugs, but that night I found a hidden stash in our bedroom. I was shocked and angry. I'd trusted Trina and didn't want to believe she and her father were both a part of what was going on."

"Then what happened?" Alex asked, when Stephan paused.

"I showed her the drugs and she went a little crazy. She told me that she had to leave, right away. She needed to take Cody over to Shelby's place." Stephan swallowed hard. "That was the last time I saw her alive."

Shelby felt sick but forced herself to ignore the sensation as she glanced at Alex. "But she didn't come straight to my place."

"What time did she leave?" Alex wanted to know.

"After midnight, maybe close to one," Stephan admitted.

"She didn't call me until four in the morning," she said, glancing at Alex. "Someone must have confronted her after she left Stephan, but before she called me. Why would she go to the shipyard with Cody in the backseat of her car?"

"Good question." Alex turned toward Stephan. "Did you see anyone else that night?"

"No. But I did call the police. I couldn't trust Trina to do the right thing, so I made the call." Stephan's face twisted with remorse. "Only I was too late. Maybe if I'd have called earlier, the minute I suspected something was going on, Trina would still be alive today."

"And you told all of this to the police?" Alex persisted.

Stephan gave a grim nod. "I had to. They were looking at me as a suspect. Only once they found out about the drugs, they closed her case. The official theory is that someone shot Trina because she stole their drugs. And they believe the shooter took all her jewelry as partial payment for the missing heroin."

TWELVE

Alex took Shelby's hand in his, giving it a warning squeeze when he saw the flash of anger in her eyes. "I'm sure the drugs didn't belong to Trina," he said quickly before she could respond. "I think someone found out Trina was leaking information to us, and they hid the drugs in her room to cast suspicion on her."

Stephan paled. "Is that what happened to her? She was killed because she wanted to help by giving information to the Feds?"

"I'm afraid so." Alex didn't like Stephan much. And he really, really didn't like the guy's attitude toward Cody. So what if the boy wasn't his biological son? After spending the past four years with him, Stephan should have cared about Cody a little. Instead, he was trying to dump the kid onto Shelby before Trina had been given a proper burial.

A stab of guilt tightened his gut. Hadn't he been tempted to do the same thing? Hand Cody over to Shelby because she'd made it clear how much she loved him? He swallowed hard and pushed his personal feelings aside to turn his attention to Stephan Kirkland and the matter at hand.

"I thought she might be guilty." Stephan looked shocked. And slightly embarrassed for thinking the worst.

"She wasn't," Alex said. He leaned forward, planting his elbows on the table. "Okay, here's how this is going to work. You are not going to tell anyone about this meeting, understand?" Alex pinned Stephan with a fierce gaze. "If anyone asks, you have not seen me or Shelby. Especially Shelby. You can say you've been trying to get in touch with her but she's not returning your phone calls. Got it?"

Stephan gave a terse nod.

"And if you're smart, you'll start looking for another line of work."

"What do you mean?" Stephan asked, shooting worried glances between Shelby and Alex. "Why do I have to look for another line of work? The marina isn't involved in anything illegal, right? The drugs were only in the shipyard."

Shelby stared at Stephan in shock. "Is that why you married my sister? For the marina?"

"No, of course not." Stephan flushed beet red and Alex suspected Shelby's question was closer to the truth than Stephan wanted to admit. "But I've dedicated my life to the marina. I'm not just going to walk away. Besides, if Russ Jacobson is going down, my skills will be needed to keep the marina running smoothly."

Alex shrugged. He'd done his duty. Stephan's decisions were his own. "Don't say I didn't warn you."

Stephan glanced at Shelby. "So you'll keep Cody? Is there any paperwork I have to sign? Do you want to stop by to pick up his things?"

"There isn't any paperwork. Trina told me that she

didn't list you as Cody's father, so you're off the hook," Shelby said in a low voice.

"And no, she's not going to stop by. He doesn't need anything from you," Alex added dismissively. "I'll provide whatever Cody needs."

Stephan narrowed his gaze. "He's your son," he accused.

He didn't bother to deny it. "Get out of here," he said, gesturing toward the door. "And remember, not a word about this meeting to anyone."

"Don't worry, I don't want to be involved in this mess any more than I already am," Stephan said with a trace of bitterness as he slid out from the booth. "Take care, Shelby."

"Goodbye, Stephan."

Alex glanced over at Logan, who'd finished his meal. At Alex's nod, Logan tossed a handful of bills on the table to cover his tab and strode after Stephan, following him outside.

"Heroin," Shelby whispered in a tortured tone. "I can't believe heroin is being smuggled on my father's ships."

He understood what a shock it must have been, to hear the awful details of what had happened to Trina right before she was killed. If he could have sheltered Shelby from the harsh reality of drug smuggling, he would have. But it was too late now. "Try to remember how Trina was working to help us," he murmured.

"I know," she said in a strangled tone. She clasped her hands tightly in her lap. "Can we leave? I want to see Cody. I need to see Cody."

"Stay here for a few more minutes," he warned when

she pushed against him, indicating she wanted to get out. "When Logan returns it will be safe for us to leave."

He could tell she was barely hanging on to her composure as they waited for Logan. When Alex saw his partner signal from the other side of the door, he slid out of the booth and offered a hand to Shelby.

She accepted his hand, her cold, clammy fingers tightening around his in a death grip. She stumbled a bit as she followed him out of the restaurant. Feeling helpless, wishing there was something he could do to make her feel better, he led the way outside.

Shelby might be in shock now, but this was nothing compared to what she was going to go through if it turned out her father really was the mastermind behind the drug running operation.

"Alex, my man, we have new intel on Marilyn, the mystery woman," Logan said when he finally met up with them back at the hotel room.

Several hours had passed since they'd finished their meeting with Stephan Kirkland. Shelby seemed to be avoiding Alex, choosing instead to focus her energy on entertaining Cody with simple card games.

Alex wished he knew what she was thinking, but he was unable to read any hint of the thoughts going on behind her shadowed blue eyes. He dragged his gaze back to Rafe and Logan, who were both watching him curiously.

"You have an ID for her?" he asked. He was almost grateful when Shelby's head snapped up to glance in their direction. He'd been concerned when she'd remained so distant and withdrawn.

"Yes, we do. Her real name is Roberta Gerard and

she's originally from New York," Logan announced reading from his notes. "Roberta's quite the interesting lady. She was married to a Joseph Allenburg, a rich old guy who was thirty years her senior. When he died rather unexpectedly, Roberta was arrested for suspicion of murder. But she was eventually released, all charges dropped when the autopsy revealed Joseph Allenburg died of natural causes."

"So she makes a habit of marrying older men, but doesn't necessarily do anything to hasten their demise," Rafe mused.

"That we know of," Alex muttered darkly. He wouldn't put anything past her.

"That's not all," Logan spoke up. "Her criminal record before that marriage, which lasted about two years, also includes being arrested for prostitution, possession of heroin and selling drugs." Logan shrugged. "Could be she decided marrying old men was an easier way to make money. Or she's more involved in the drug smuggling than we realized."

"So it's possible she's in on the whole thing. The timing fits. She came to Green Bay right about the time when drugs started showing up on the ships. Maybe marrying a rich guy like Russ Jacobson was icing on the cake." Alex glanced at Shelby who had grown pale as they discussed possible theories. "So who is she working with? Is it a mere coincidence that she left Russ the same day Bobby Drake showed up dead? And why was she meeting Mayor Flynn at the pub, looking upset?"

"We can try showing Cody the mayor's picture, see if he recognizes him," Logan drawled. "If he's the bad guy, then we'll know how she's involved. The two of them could be in on it together."

"Yeah, or else she was involved with Bobby Drake and is worried about her own fate now that he's dead. Or she could be involved with someone else that we haven't thought of yet." Alex let out a deep, heavy sigh. "All right. Let's show Cody the picture. See what happens."

Rafe and Logan glanced at each other and nodded. Rafe pulled out a newspaper article. "I have a photograph right here. It's a close-up of the mayor's face."

Alex took the photograph and smoothed it out on the table. Shelby and Cody had just completed their game of Go Fish. "Cody? Would you come here for a minute?"

"Sure." Cody eagerly scrambled to his feet. Shelby followed, her expression grim.

He understood her trepidation and tried to smile reassuringly. He pulled Cody onto his lap and tapped the picture on the table. "Do you know this guy?"

Cody scrunched up his face and shook his head. "No."

Alex frowned. "Are you sure?"

Cody nodded. "I'm sure. Will you play cards with us?" he asked, his attention clearly not on the photograph.

"Ah, maybe in a little while." He glanced at Rafe and Logan who both shrugged. Cody either hadn't seen the bad guy's face or the mayor wasn't involved.

But that didn't leave Marilyn off the hook.

Alex threaded his hands through his hair in sheer frustration. There had to be a way to break this case open. There just had to be.

"Cody, why don't you go play in your room for a while?" Shelby said softly.

Alex glanced over, noticing Cody looked like he

might argue, but the boy finally did as he was told. He slid off his lap, landing on the floor. She waited until he was in the other room before turning toward him. "If you suspect Marilyn is involved, doesn't that mean my father is innocent?"

"I don't know, Shelby." He stared at her for a moment. The threads of this case were so tangled, he couldn't be absolutely sure of anything. "Maybe. For your sake, I hope he is innocent. Obviously he's not Cody's bad man. And I will admit, I can't imagine Russ Jacobson giving the order to have his own daughter murdered."

"Exactly." Shelby's tone was full of satisfaction. "It's very easy for me to believe Marilyn is guilty. I never liked her much anyway. And the more I think about her being involved with Cody's bad man, the more I'm convinced my father could be innocent."

Alex wished he could agree. "Or maybe your father discovered she was involved in the drug smuggling but kept quiet because he loved her."

Shelby's eyes narrowed. "Why do you insist on believing the worst about him? I thought we just agreed he'd never harm Trina?"

Alex glanced away. His gut instincts weren't easy to explain. He just didn't have a good feeling about Jacobson.

Rafe spoke up. "I think we have to consider that Cody's bad man might have been working on his own, crossing the line when he attacked Trina."

Alex followed the line of Rafe's logic. "Which means, it's possible Jacobson is the ringleader, and knows who's guilty of killing his daughter. If that's true, then maybe Trina's death means the plan has changed and now he's going to pin the whole operation on the murderer." Abruptly, the puzzle pieces fell nicely into place. "Taking Marilyn down with him."

He heard Shelby suck in a harsh breath. He wanted to go to her, to put a supporting arm around her shoulders. Yet despite their almost kiss earlier that afternoon, he knew his presence wouldn't be welcome.

Not anymore.

Everything had changed after the meeting with Stephan. For the first time, Shelby was being forced to seriously consider her father's guilt. Even Stephan had believed Jacobson to be involved in the drug smuggling. And there was nothing Alex could say to soften the blow.

She might claim her father wasn't a murderer, but in his opinion, anyone helping to put drugs into the hands of children was exactly that. A murderer. His best friend Toby's death was only one example. There were hundreds and thousands more.

Alex curled the fingers of his injured hand, flexing the damaged muscles. He planned on bringing the man responsible to justice. He'd do whatever was necessary to break the cycle of drugs and death. Even arrest Shelby's only living parent.

Yet he also knew, no matter how unfair it was, that if he did so, Shelby would always look at him as the man who'd arrested her father and Cody's grandfather.

Seeking justice could mean losing the woman he was beginning to fall in love with.

Shelby sat by Cody's side long after he'd fallen asleep. Despite her own bone-weary exhaustion, her mind kept replaying the conversation with Stephan over and over in her mind.

Finally she knelt beside her bed, and opened her heart and her mind to prayer.

Heavenly Father, help me to see the truth, Your truth. If my father is guilty of this horrible crime, give me the strength to do whatever is necessary to keep us all safe. Please, Lord, guide Alex, too. Help him to keep his mind open to all possibilities. I trust You, Lord, to show him the way. Amen.

With her heart and her soul at peace, she finally slept.

The next morning, she awoke early, feeling well rested and anxious to do something. Being in the hotel suite with Alex and Rafe made her feel safe. But since Trina's funeral wasn't until tomorrow, she feared the day would drag by excruciatingly slow.

Silently, so she wouldn't wake Cody, she washed up in the bathroom and then paused near the doorway leading into the general living area. She could hear two male voices talking. She knew it was wrong to eavesdrop, but couldn't help herself when she heard her name.

"Shelby's never going to forgive me," Alex said.

"You underestimate her faith, my friend," Rafe countered. "She knows you don't mean her any harm."

"Yeah." Alex let out a harsh sound. "But that doesn't exactly change the outcome, now, does it? I'm hurting her even though I don't mean to."

"If her father is guilty, he's the one at fault," Rafe pointed out. "Not you."

"It doesn't matter much either way. I'm still the guy who's going to help bring him down." Alex's agonized tone wrenched her heart.

Shame washed over her, causing her to turn away from the doorway. She'd been so upset about the recent turn in events that she'd misled Alex into believing she blamed him. And she knew very well that none of this was his fault. She'd come to him for help and he'd gone above and beyond, especially during the snowstorm. It was her own problem if her father happened to be involved.

She took a step toward Alex, wanting to go to him, to reassure him that she didn't blame him at all, when Cody cried out in his sleep.

"Mama!" Shelby hurried to his side, where he thrashed around in the bed. "Mama!"

"Shh, Cody. It's okay. I'm here with you," she crooned, gathering him close so he wouldn't hurt himself with his flailing arms and legs.

He continued to cry, so she rocked him in her arms, murmuring words of comfort. She wasn't surprised when the door opened farther and Alex stood in the doorway.

"Is he all right?" Alex asked, his expression mirroring his concern.

"He had another nightmare," she explained, although no doubt Alex figured that one out for himself. "I'm sure he'll be fine."

He hesitated in the doorway, as if loath to leave them alone. "Do you really think attending the funeral will help?"

"According to Dr. Zander it will. But you know as well as I do, there are no guarantees. And I need to know you'll think of a way to keep him safe."

He nodded, and stood awkwardly for a moment. "Is there anything I can do?"

Her heart squeezed for a moment, as she saw a hint of longing reflected in his eyes. Alex wanted to be a father to Cody, but he didn't know how. She'd gladly let him step in right now, but Cody's emotional state was still fragile, and he didn't know Alex well enough to find comfort with him.

"Is there something for breakfast?" she asked.

"Instant oatmeal, since Cody claimed apple cinnamon was his favorite."

"We'll be out in a few minutes," she promised.

Alex nodded and finally moved away from the doorway, leaving them alone. Once she'd gotten Cody calmed down from his dream, she helped him brush his teeth and change his clothes.

Alex, Logan and Rafe were all in the kitchen area when she emerged from the bedroom. They greeted both her and Cody.

When they finished eating breakfast, she urged Cody to watch cartoons for a bit, sensing the men were on a mission. Sure enough, once she'd cleared the table of their dishes—it still made her chuckle to watch all of the men eating Cody's oatmeal—they took over.

Rafe took a sheet of Cody's drawing paper and quickly drew bold strokes across the page. "Here's the intersection the church is on. And here are all the doorways leading in and out of the building."

"There are too many entry points," Alex said, groaning and throwing up his hands in frustration. "How are we supposed to keep an eye on all four?"

"We don't." Rafe's calmness only seemed to grate on Alex's nerves. "Shelby and Cody will only go in and out of the main entrance, here. From this vantage point across the street, you can keep an eye on both of these doorways." Rafe marked them in blue. "Logan and I will be inside with Shelby and Cody. No one is likely to make a move on her or the boy in the middle of a crowded funeral."

Alex scowled. "You don't know what this guy is capable of doing. What if he knocks her unconscious and drags her out the back?" Alex seemed bent on poking holes in their plan.

"You mean after he's managed to get past both me and Rafe?" Logan asked with a loud snort. "Don't think so."

She moved closer, realizing she was a big part of this plan. "I can tell you what the inside of the church looks like," she offered.

Rafe flashed his blindingly white smile. "Thanks, *amiga,* but I know what the inside of this church looks like. We checked it out earlier this morning."

"Of course you did," she murmured, blushing a bit. "Sorry, I should have known." She glanced at the drawing in the center of the table. "Why have you decided to keep Alex outside?" she asked, curiously.

The three men exchanged a long look.

"We feel it's safer for Alex to stay outside," Logan offered.

She paled and glanced at Alex who was scowling again. "Safer?"

"Shelby, we've decided it's best if Rafe accompanies you and Cody to the funeral," Alex explained.

A cold chill snaked down her back and she crossed her arms over her chest to hide how she was feeling. "I don't understand. You went to the meeting with Stephan with me. What's the difference?"

"For one thing, I haven't been fully cleared to get back in the field, and there's no guarantee that my shooting will be accurate enough," he said. "And besides that, being attacked proves my cover was blown. Even though I look much different now, I don't want the members of your family, or even Mayor Flynn for that matter, to get a good look at me." Steel determination lined Alex's gaze. "I'll be stationed outside as backup, well within reach if you need anything."

"As a member of the coast guard, I'm the most recognizable of the bunch," Rafe added. "The plan is for you to introduce me as your new boyfriend. I'm going to stay glued to your side and Cody's the entire time."

"And Logan?" she asked, looking at the newest agent.

"He's going to mingle as one of Trina's friends," Alex said. "We're hoping your father doesn't notice him much. We figure there are bound to be people there, friends of Trina, who your father won't know."

She blinked, trying to take it all in. They'd planned all this out in such a short time. Yet while she was sure the plans were solid, she hadn't realized how much she'd been counting on Alex to be there with her. "Is it really necessary to introduce Rafe as my boyfriend?" she said finally. "I don't like lying, no offense, Rafe."

Rafe chuckled. "None taken. How about you simply introduce me as the new man in your life? Technically, that's true. I'm one of three new men in your life." He waved his arm wide, including the others.

She supposed stretching the truth that much wouldn't hurt. "All right."

"Okay, now that we have that settled, let's get back to the entrances." Alex tapped on the paper in the center of the table, frowning. "I don't know. I still don't like it. Let's just say that somehow you both lose Shelby in the crowd and someone comes behind her with a gun.

If they force her out the back doorway, we wouldn't know until it was too late. It's too big of a risk."

"Remember, he'd have to get past both of us," Logan said with a long-drawn-out sigh. At Alex's dark look he shrugged. "But okay, let's say you're right. Rafe and I both lose Shelby at the exact moment someone approaches her from behind. What if we put together some sort of time frame? Say an hour? If Shelby and Cody don't come out through the main doorway in an hour, you go in after them."

"An hour? Are you kidding me?" Alex pushed away from the table in a fit of disgust. "By then, they could easily be dead."

THIRTEEN

Alex knew he was probably overreacting, but he didn't like the idea of Shelby and Cody being exposed to danger. He couldn't seem to shake the bad feeling that nagged at him, ever since he'd put the pieces of the puzzle together about Shelby's father.

He was keenly aware of the way Logan and Rafe exchanged a concerned glance when they thought he wasn't looking. They no doubt thought he was too emotionally involved to be of any use to them.

Maybe they were right. He dragged a hand through his hair. It was difficult to remain cool and objective when Shelby's and Cody's lives were in danger.

"Forget the time-frame angle. If we lose sight of Shelby, we'll send you a text message," Rafe said, breaking the strained silence.

Since he couldn't come up with anything better, he nodded. "Fine. A text message will have to be good enough." It wasn't as if he didn't trust Rafe and Logan, but he'd prefer to be the one inside, next to her.

Shelby glanced at him too, her gaze full of concern. As if she was worried about him, rather than the other way around. He had to get a grip, or he wouldn't be any good to anyone.

He hid the depth of his fear behind an indifferent mask. "What time does the funeral service start?"

"Visitation starts at four in the afternoon," Rafe announced, reading from the obituary he'd picked up. "Followed by a brief prayer service at five-thirty."

"I'd like to stay for the prayer service," Shelby said.

He nodded. "I know. Should be fine."

"We could get the local authorities involved, requesting extra security for the back exits," Logan said, staring at Rafe's sketch.

"No." Alex's bold refusal caused more raised eyebrows. "No local cops. We can't rule out the possibility of someone working from inside."

"Do you really think so?" Logan asked.

"Someone tracked us to Kayla's bed-and-breakfast. The only two calls that we made, outside of Rafe, was the call I made to the local police and the one Shelby made to her father."

"I called the day care center, too," Shelby reminded him.

"Cartoons are over," Cody called out, interrupting them from where he was seated in the living room. Alex glanced over to see the boy was jumping up and down on the sofa.

"Cody, get down from there." The boy stared at him defiantly, continuing to jump, adding fuel to Alex's temper. "I said get down!"

Cody's eyes widened with fear and he immediately stopped, his face crumpling as he started to cry. Alex mentally winced, knowing he'd been too harsh. For a moment he'd sounded just like his father.

A really bad comparison.

"Cody, that's not how we sit on the furniture," Shelby said in a soothing voice, as she crossed over to Cody, gathering him into her arms. "If you fall off, you could hit your head."

Alex hated knowing he'd scared Cody and stepped forward. "Do you want to see my scar?" he asked, kneeling down by the sofa where they were seated. "I was jumping on my mom's bed and hit my head on the edge of the frame. Got five stitches right here," he tapped the diagonal scar half-buried in his right eyebrow.

Cody's expression cleared as he gently fingered the mark on Alex's forehead. "Did it hurt?"

Alex nodded. "Not any more, but at the time I cried and cried." He almost added more detail about the blood, but then remembered Cody's extreme reaction to his injured hand. "That's why I corrected you. I didn't want you to be hurt like I was."

Cody jammed his fingers in his mouth and nodded.

Crisis averted, at least for the moment. But those moments when he'd lost his temper, sounding too much like his father, bothered him for a long time afterward.

Alex couldn't seem to relax, even after he'd escorted Shelby and Cody to the local department store so they could pick up the proper clothing to wear for Trina's funeral. The brief outing had helped to get Cody out of the hotel suite for a while, but Alex had been tense and nervous the entire time.

Long after Shelby and Cody had gone to bed, he sat in the kitchenette area, too keyed up to sleep.

When Shelby opened the door from her bedroom, he

glanced up in surprise. "Can't sleep either?" he asked in a low voice.

"No. Figured I'd try some herbal tea," she said, clenching the sash of her robe tightly at her waist. "Would you like some?"

He grimaced and then nodded. "Sure. Why not?"

She heated two mugs of water in the microwave. After putting a tea bag in each, she carried them to the table. "You're really worried about this funeral, aren't you?"

He stared into his cup for a moment. "I shouldn't be worried. The funeral is a public place and it's not likely anyone will try something shady with all those people around."

"But you're still worried," she persisted.

"Yeah. I guess I am."

She reached over to cover his hand with hers. "Maybe you need to try putting your faith in God, Alex. You, Rafe and Logan have prepared as much as you can. I've prayed about this too, and I believe we are meant to attend Trina's funeral. From here on out, the future is God's will."

He offered a faint smile. "Guess I still have a lot to learn about being a Christian, don't I?"

She didn't move her hand and he turned his so that their palms were meshed together, their fingers interlaced. "You're doing fine. All you need to do is believe in our Lord."

"Yeah." He took a sip of the tea, which wasn't as bad as he'd anticipated. "I think the hardest part is realizing I'm not the one in control."

"We certainly control our actions and our thoughts, but I believe everything outside our control happens for a reason," Shelby gently pointed out. "Helps to talk about it and to pray."

"I'll keep that in mind." He took another sip of his tea. She'd finished hers, setting her empty mug aside.

"Good night, Alex," she said tugging on her hand and rising to her feet.

He didn't immediately let go of her hand, but stood and leaned close, brushing a gentle kiss along her cheek, so he wouldn't scare her. "Good night, Shelby."

Shyly, she reached up and brushed her mouth against his, a soft caress that was over before he knew it yet still made his breath catch in his throat. The kiss was over far too soon. "See you in the morning," she murmured.

He let her go, even though he wanted very much to hold her close. But he told himself to be patient. Shelby's kiss had been her way of telling him that she wasn't afraid. At least not of him.

And her trust was definitely worth waiting for.

Shelby was glad when the time came to prepare for Trina's funeral. Sitting in this hotel room was already driving her crazy.

After they'd gotten safely through the funeral, she and Cody would go back to the hotel with Alex, while Rafe and Logan did their best to uncover the mastermind of the drug smuggling operation. Apparently they'd discovered some secret gambling debts Mayor Flynn was hiding and as a result, he'd moved back up a few notches on their suspect list.

She took a deep breath when Rafe pulled into the church parking lot. "Are you ready?" he asked, flashing his bright smile.

"Yes." She glanced back at Cody, who'd been un-characteristically silent on the way over, since she'd explained what to expect at church and the somberness of the occasion. "Are you ready, Cody?"

He nodded.

She reached for the door handle, and then stopped and looked at Rafe. "Wait. I need to know your last name, so I can introduce you to my father."

"DeSilva. My name is Rafe DeSilva."

She repeated the name, committing it to memory. She stepped from the car and opened the rear door, for Cody.

"I'm scared," he said, his lower lip trembling.

"Oh, sweetheart, church isn't scary. We're going into God's house. He's going to be watching over us the whole time."

He seemed to hesitate, but then allowed her to unlatch his toddler seat so she could lift him from the car. Instead of setting him on his feet, though, she kept him in her arms.

"Everything okay?" Rafe murmured.

"Fine." She reminded herself that Dr. Zander thought it was good for Cody to have closure, so she walked into the church, feeling a sense of peace the minute she entered the sanctuary. The place was already crowded and several people approached her, offering condolences. Once Cody seemed to adjust to his surroundings, she set him on his feet.

She finally caught sight of her father and he quickly made his way over. "Shelby." He leaned down to kiss her cheek, and then ruffled Cody's hair affectionately. "How's my favorite grandson?"

"Hi, Grandpa." Cody's apprehension seemed to vanish.

"It's good to see you, Dad." Shelby wet her suddenly dry lips and pulled Rafe forward. "I'd like to introduce you to a very special friend, Rafe DeSilva. Rafe, this is my father, Russ Jacobson."

Rafe held out his hand and her father took it solemnly. "Rafe DeSilva. I recognize that name. Didn't I just read something about you in the paper?"

Rafe nodded and slipped a steadying arm around Shelby's waist. "Yes, sir. I'm with the ninth district coast guard. You might have read about how we rescued those ice fishermen off the bay a few weeks ago."

Shelby thought her father appeared taken aback by that news. "You're with the coast guard?" he asked.

A chill snaked down her spine and her smile slipped. Rafe must have noticed because he gave her a reassuring squeeze. "Yes, sir, for the past seven years," Rafe said proudly.

Her father didn't seem at all happy. "How did you and Shelby meet?"

"My nephew attends her day care center."

Shelby was glad they were standing together, so they'd have their story straight. She didn't understand how Alex could work undercover.

If she didn't know better, she'd think Rafe was thoroughly enjoying himself. "It took me a while, but I finally convinced Shelby to go out with me. God was watching over me, I think."

Shelby returned his smile, pretending that her father's discomfort didn't bother her.

"Hmm." Her father continued to look uneasy, but just then a group of relatives arrived, his cousins that she didn't know very well, so she moved away and took the opportunity to kneel beside Cody, straightening his shirt beneath his vest. "How are you doing?"

"Okay." His gaze was serious. "Is it time to say goodbye now?"

Assailed by a barrage of doubts, she hesitated. Maybe she shouldn't push him. "Is that all right with you?"

He nodded.

"We'll say goodbye together, then." She took his hand and ignoring Rafe for a moment, led Cody over to the front of the church. She knelt beside the casket and Cody followed suit.

She clasped his hand. "Dear Lord, we ask You to keep my sister and Cody's mom at Your side in heaven. We will miss her here on earth but we know she's in a much better place with You. Please help us to be strong. We loved her so much," her voice broke and she fumbled for a tissue. "Rest in peace, Trina," she said softly.

"I'm glad you're in heaven now," Cody whispered. "Goodbye, Mama. I love you."

When she and Cody finished praying for Trina, she led him away so others could approach. She was surprised when Rafe was the next in line, kneeling to offer a brief prayer for Trina as well, before coming back to join them.

She blew her nose and he enveloped her in a warm hug. It was nice, but at that moment, she missed Alex. Reminding herself that Alex's safety was more important than her needs, she took hold of Cody's hand and led him through the crowd toward the back of the church.

Suddenly she heard Cody gasp.

She froze, glancing around in alarm. "What is it?" she asked.

"I saw him." Cody's eyes were brilliant green orbs, dominating his small face.

"Who?" she asked, even though she was very much afraid she knew.

"The bad man." Cody pointed through the milling crowd with a small chubby finger. "Over there."

Rafe swiftly swung Cody into his arms, so that his face was next to Rafe's. "Where? Show me the bad man, Cody."

Cody clutched Rafe tightly around the neck. "I don't know. I saw him, over there somewhere."

"But not now?" Rafe persisted, slowly moving from side to side so Cody could get a good look around. She scanned the crowd herself, looking for anyone who might match Cody's description.

"He's gone," Cody whispered, burying his face into Rafe's neck.

"Don't worry about it," Rafe soothed, rubbing a hand over Cody's back. "If you see him again, let me know, okay?"

Rafe carried Cody in his arms until he relaxed and wiggled to be let free. Rafe set him on his feet and Shelby kept Cody's hand in hers, unwilling to let him get too far.

Logan approached. "All right?" he asked.

Rafe nodded. "Cody thought he saw the bad man, but he's gone now."

Logan scanned the crowd. "There are a lot of people who could fit the description. I saw the Mayor talking to Russ Jacobson. Neither one of them seemed very happy."

"Maybe my father is still upset about Marilyn," Shelby pointed out.

"Could be," Logan drawled. "I overheard the mayor and your father saying something about Bobby Drake. I got the impression that Marilyn had gone to the Mayor about Bobby's death, but I can't say for sure."

She felt sick at the thought of Marilyn cheating on her father with a rough guy like Bobby Drake. "Where is she?"

Logan shrugged. "Haven't seen her around at all, which is odd considering she and Jacobson aren't divorced yet. I'd expect her to be here."

Shelby thought Marilyn's absence was strange, too.

"My pager is going off," Rafe said. "I'm not on call except as emergency backup, so I have to answer this. Don't go too far," he warned moving a few feet away for privacy.

Stephan chose that moment to approach and Logan drifted away. "Shelby, your father wants to talk to you when you have a minute." Stephan glanced down at Cody. "Alone."

"Why?" She tightened her grip on Cody's hand. She wasn't going anywhere without Cody.

Stephan shrugged. "He didn't say, but I get the feeling he's not too keen on your new boyfriend."

If Stephan wondered where Alex was, he didn't mention anything. A gnawing concern filled her stomach. Was Alex right that her father had been protecting Marilyn all along? It was possible now that Marilyn had left him that her father was looking for a way to tell the authorities without condemning himself.

And if so, she knew she'd offer to help.

Rafe was still on the phone, so she glanced around looking for her father. When she saw him standing beside the front door, he caught her gaze and gestured her forward. Hesitantly, she glanced over at Logan, who stood only a few feet away, chatting with someone she didn't know.

Swinging Cody into her arms, she walked toward her father. She didn't doubt that Logan would keep an eye on her. And Alex was outside, watching the main entrance. All she needed was a few minutes alone with her father.

If he was in trouble, she'd beg him to turn himself in.

Alex slouched against the side of the building across the street from the church, stamping his feet in the cold and remembering only too well why he hated stakeouts.

Interestingly enough, he'd noted that Marilyn hadn't bothered to show up at the funeral. In his mind, that only added to his suspicions. The mayor was there, along with several members of the Green Bay police including the Chief of Police, Benjamin Wallace. Seems like Jacobson had an important standing in the community.

From where he stood watching the various men walking into the church, many of them could have fit Cody's description of the bad man.

The main doors opened and he saw Russ Jacobson emerge from the building. Alex frowned and glanced at his watch. Odd, that Jacobson would leave his daughter's funeral early. Especially before the prayer service.

His heart froze in his chest, when the door opened again and Shelby walked outside, holding Cody in her arms. Without any sign of Rafe or Logan, she fell into step beside her father, following the winding sidewalk, as if she didn't have a care in the world.

FOURTEEN

Alex clenched his fingers into fists, a ball of fear clogging his throat. What was she doing? Had she lost her mind? Any minute he expected her to stop, turn around and go back inside, but instead Shelby, Cody and her father took the pathway leading all the way down to the street, talking earnestly.

He had no idea how Shelby managed to get out of the church without either Rafe or Logan noticing her departure. He quickly texted messages to each of them, as he ducked over to the building next door, trying to follow the rambling path Shelby and her father made.

Jacobson gestured toward the marina located just a few blocks down the street with one hand, and he imagined the old man was trying to convince Shelby to go with him, but Shelby stopped walking and shook her head, holding Cody to her side.

"That's it, Shelby," Alex muttered to himself, as he stayed in the shadows, out of sight. "Don't trust him. And don't leave the area around the church."

But then she moved forward, walking up to meet her father, and the three of them took the sidewalk that led down to the marina. He wished he could tell what

Shelby was saying to her father as they walked, their heads bent toward each other deep in conversation, but he couldn't.

Maybe she was trying to convince her father to give himself up to the authorities. The very idea made him sweat. She might not understand the magnitude of danger, but he did.

He didn't trust Russ Jacobson. Not even knowing he loved his daughter and grandson.

Turn around, Shelby. Go back to the sanctuary of the church, he silently pleaded.

He took several deep breaths to calm his racing heart. She wasn't far from the church and Logan and Rafe would be there soon. Remembering what Shelby had said about putting his faith in the Lord, he murmured a quick prayer as he followed them down to the marina.

Heavenly Father, please keep Shelby and Cody safe.

Shelby and her father paused near the main building of the marina, deserted for the most part this time of the year. There was only a sliver of moon in the sky as darkness fell. Alex took a chance, crossing the street to get closer to the marina. When he reached the building, he stayed along the side, creeping closer until he could overhear what Shelby and her father were saying.

"Okay, Dad, you've told me your concerns about Marilyn. And I'm sorry she cleaned out your joint bank account."

"I was a fool," Jacobson muttered.

To her credit, Shelby didn't comment. "Marilyn wasn't just unfaithful, though, was she? Come on, Dad. I want to hear the truth from you. The truth about the drugs."

"Drugs?" Jacobson's voice sounded surprised. "Shelby, how in the world do you know about the drugs?"

"I tried to tell you, I know what's going on. And furthermore, we're pretty sure Marilyn is involved in the drug smuggling, too. But Dad, it's not too late. You still have a chance. You need to turn yourself in and tell them everything!" she pleaded urgently.

Alex risked a quick glance around the corner to see Jacobson shaking his head.

"No, Shelby," he said firmly. "Not yet. I need more time to clear my name."

"There isn't enough time," Shelby insisted.

"You should listen to your daughter, Jacobson." A deep voice came out of the darkness, from farther behind them. Alex froze for a moment, until the figure came closer. A tall man dressed in a dark blue cop uniform stepped out of the shadows, and when he saw the man's face, he felt a wave of relief.

Lieutenant Eric Holden, Rafe's contact within the Green Bay police department.

"Shelby, take Cody and get out of here, now!" her father commanded.

Shelby reached for Cody, but before she could move, Holden leveled his weapon, aiming directly at them. "Nobody move."

Alex stared in shock. What was Holden thinking? He should know better than to aim his weapon at civilians.

"Step away from your father, Shelby," Holden continued, his gun never wavering. "I don't want you or Cody to get hurt."

"I'm the one you want, leave her alone," Jacobson said, in a voice accustomed to being obeyed.

"Dad? I don't understand—" Shelby glanced between the two men, obviously confused. Eric Holden took a few steps toward her and she didn't move away from the man who represented the law.

"I'm sorry you had to see this, Shelby," Holden said in a placating tone. "Especially on the night we're honoring your sister's memory. But I have to tell you, your father is under arrest for drug smuggling and murder. Your father's wife, Marilyn, is dead. And we have irrefutable proof, Jacobson, that you killed her. You might as well turn yourself in. There's no escape, not any more."

Shelby gasped, her eyes widening in horror. Alex watched the scene unfold. This was the moment he'd been training for, taking out the mastermind behind the drug smuggling operation. But something wasn't quite right. He held his weapon firmly in his left hand, in case Shelby's father decided to make a run for it.

His gaze dropped to Cody. The stark horror etched on his son's face made him freeze. His son was staring at Eric Holden, as if he were seeing a ghost.

Or the bad man of his nightmares.

And suddenly he knew. The bandage on the side of Holden's temple confirmed it. He was the one who had attacked Trina. It had been him all along. No wonder they couldn't crack the case. Holden, Rafe's contact, was running the drug smuggling ring. And from the looks of things, he was right now setting up Shelby's father to take the fall. For Marilyn's murder. And for the drugs. The same way he'd arranged for heroin to be found in Trina's bedroom.

Just like he'd arranged for Alex to be attacked, when he'd gotten too close to the truth.

"Grandpa!" Cody shouted, darting away from Holden and running toward Jacobson.

"Cody, no!" Shelby cried out trying to follow. But it was too late. Jacobson grabbed Cody, hauling him out of harm's way, but Eric Holden grabbed at Shelby. She slipped away, running toward the docks, hiding in the shadows of the boats that were suspended high above the water.

Alex was tempted to fire, but didn't want to let Holden know he was there. When Russ Jacobson ducked around the far corner of the building, carrying Cody out of harm's way, Holden disappeared, taking off after Shelby. The stalemate was broken by the knowledge that Shelby would want him to see his—their—son.

Alex peered through the night, his heart thundering in his chest, trying to figure out where he'd gone. He was faced with an impossible decision. Staying here to ensure his son's safety or going after Shelby.

After long tense seconds, he headed around the opposite side, to meet up with Jacobson and Cody.

Silently praying. *Lord, keep Shelby safe.*

When Eric Holden had nearly grabbed her, Shelby had almost collapsed in fear. In order to save Cody, she'd kicked off her useless pumps and ran.

Visions of the gunman chasing Trina flashed in her mind. Maybe this was God's plan all along, for her to live her final moments the way Trina had before she'd died. Trina had given up her life when she'd drawn the gunman away from Cody. And Shelby was willing to sacrifice herself to do the same.

Her father's yacht, the *Juliet,* offered some protection

as she darted into the boat's shadow. Tonight, the darkness wasn't something to fear. It offered protection.

She held her breath, straining to listen. She'd noticed Cody's reation to Lieutenant Holden, so she knew he must be Cody's bad guy. He'd murdered Marilyn and Trina, too. She'd be more afraid if not for the fact she knew Alex had likely followed them down to the marina.

Alex would protect his son.

Strangely enough, she wasn't as worried about herself. Her normal fear of the dark vanished. She knew God was with her.

She inched down around to the front of the boat. The sound of metal scraping against metal made her hold her breath, unsure which way to move. She waited, her eyes searching the darkness, struggling to come up with a plan.

She needed to head farther north, to put more distance between Eric Holden and Cody. Surely Rafe and Logan would have arrived to help by now.

All she needed was a little more time.

Her feet were freezing without shoes and just when she'd decided to run, a figure loomed out of the darkness.

"Gotcha," Eric said, an evil, leering grin on his face.

In a desperate move, she darted to the left, but he moved faster, grabbing her and hauling her against his hard chest. The acrid scent of cigarette smoke made her gag.

The memory of the night she was attacked swelled in her mind. She could see his face from the corner of her eye and knew. This man smelled and sounded the same. Holden! Eric Holden had attacked her two years ago.

"Don't try anything," he warned, his voice low and gravel-rough near her ear. "I have a gun." He put the cold steel to her temple, as if she needed the harsh reminder. "And this time, I'll finish the job right."

"You'll never get away with this," she said, trying to remain calm. "The DEA is on to you."

Holden momentarily tensed, his tight grip painful around her neck before he finally relaxed. "I have the law on my side. Your lovely sister figured that out pretty quick. She thought she could get away from me, the little fool."

"You killed her."

Holden didn't deny it. "That brat of hers saw me from inside the car, when she fought me off with the tire iron. I would have tracked her down and killed her for that alone. I was so close to getting away clean, but it doesn't matter."

"Why did you kill Marilyn?" she asked.

"She's nothing but a drug addict, weeping and wailing after I killed Bobby Drake. When I realized she was on the verge of ratting me out, I got rid of her."

"She met with the Mayor before she died. She probably told him all about you." It was a shot on the dark, but she knew her arrow had hit the mark, when he tensed up again.

"She couldn't have said anything. She didn't know I was involved until I killed her."

He acted like he was invincible. Shelby held herself still, swallowing her fear.

"I can get rid of you, the brat and your stupid father, and still come out of this looking like a hero. I'll set up your useless DEA agent as the guilty one. I'm a cop, I know how to plant evidence, making sure everyone will believe me."

Was Holden delusional? Did he really think he could keep killing people and get away with it? She noticed he didn't mention Rafe and Logan, and prayed that meant he didn't know about Alex's backups. Instinctively she knew she needed to buy more time. Time for Rafe and Logan to find Alex. For the three of them to get to Cody and her father. Between the three of them, they'd take Eric Holden down easily.

She wanted to live, to have a chance at a future with Alex and Cody. She'd just begun to realize how much she cared for Alex. If necessary, she'd sacrifice her life to save them both. She prayed it wouldn't come to that.

"Come on," he said harshly. Keeping his arm locked around her neck, her back against his chest and the gun pressed against her temple, Holden dragged her to the main building of the marina. She stumbled as rocks stabbed at her feet.

"Listen up, Jacobson," Holden called as he approached. "I have your daughter. Bring me the boy or I'll kill her."

Her father came out from around the corner of the marina building, holding his hands up high. She was relieved Cody was nowhere in sight. "Don't shoot. Please, don't shoot," Jacobsen pleaded.

"No!" Shelby struggled to get free, but Holden's arm tightened painfully around her neck, cutting off her airway. Red dots swam before her eyes. For a moment she feared she'd choke to death right then and there.

And while she didn't mind going home to her Lord, she did wish she'd taken the time to tell Alex how much she cared about him.

How much she loved him.

He eased up on the pressure, and she drew lifesaving oxygen into her lungs.

Soon, she'd make her move. He'd likely kill her but that didn't matter.

Dear Lord, keep Alex and Cody safe.

"What are you waiting for?" Jacobson asked in a low, harsh tone. "Shoot him already."

Deep in the shadows, Alex trained his gun on Eric Holden's face, holding his left arm steady by propping it against the building. From the corner of his eye, he noted Rafe had taken hold of Cody, trying hard to keep the boy quiet. Rafe had a wound on his head from when he'd been knocked unconscious, no doubt by Holden before he'd made his move, and he was still unsteady on his feet. Logan had gone back around to the opposite side of the marina, planning to trap Holden so that he'd have no place to run.

A bead of sweat ran down the length of Alex's spine. The situation couldn't possibly be any worse. He had a clear view of Holden's head, a shot he would normally take without thinking twice. But not now. Not like this. And absolutely not with his left hand, considering how Holden had Shelby pressed in front of him, his gun plastered to her head. Any sudden move on Alex's part might cause Holden to pull the trigger, killing her.

Alex gripped the gun, swallowing hard.

"Where's the kid?" Holden shouted. "I'll shoot her if I don't see that kid in ten seconds!"

From the corner of his eye, he saw Cody struggling in Rafe's arms. There was no possibility of risking Cody for Shelby, but Holden didn't know that. Time was running out. He knew with grim certainty Holden would shoot.

He thought about how God was watching over them. Guiding him. He took a deep breath and held it, focusing his energy on his target.

Suddenly, Shelby grabbed at Holden's arm clamped around her neck. She dug her fingernails into his flesh and sank her teeth into his arm, as well. The bold move caught Holden off guard, and he howled with rage, moving the gun away from her temple for a few precious seconds.

Praying with every fiber of his being, Alex squeezed his finger on the trigger of his weapon. Holden jerked, and his hold on Shelby broke. She dropped to the ground at his feet, covering her head with her hands. Holden aimed wild, getting a couple of shots off, aiming all over the place, including straight down at Shelby. Alex saw her body jerk and knew she'd been hit.

His gaze trained on Holden, Alex fired again and again.

Holden stumbled backward, a shocked expression on his face moments before he finally hit the ground. Alex realized he'd finally hit Holden in the center of his forehead.

If only it wasn't too late.

"Shelby!" Alex rushed over to Shelby's side, dropping to his knees, his worst fears clawing to the surface when she didn't move. His heart thundered in his ears, filling his head with a strange roaring sound. He couldn't be too late. He couldn't! He pressed his fingers against her neck, feeling for a pulse. Nearly fainted with relief when he found the thin, thready beat. "Shelby? Please don't die. Please don't die."

Urgently, he ran his hands over her body, searching for any sign of an injury. Maybe she was suffering from shock? But then his fingers stumbled upon something wet, warm and sticky.

Blood. From a small wound in the lower part of her abdomen. He balled up a fistful of her jacket, pressing it against the oozing wound.

"Call an ambulance!" he shouted, using all his weight to stem the flow of blood. "Hurry!"

"Aunt Shelby!" Cody cried. Rafe must have let him go, because the boy came running over, tears streaming down his tiny face. "Aunt Shelby!"

Alex held out a hand to his son, catching him up against him, holding him close with one arm even as he held pressure on Shelby's wound with the other. "She's alive, Cody. She's going to be okay." He wasn't sure which one of them he was trying to convince.

"Daddy," Cody wailed, burying his face into Alex's neck. "Don't leave me, Daddy!"

His heart squeezed painfully in his chest as his son called him Daddy for the first time. He turned and pressed a kiss to the top of Cody's head.

"I won't leave you," he promised. "Your aunt Shelby is going to be all right, and I will never leave you."

Cody's arms snaked around his neck, clinging tightly. Alex closed his eyes as a sudden, overwhelming surge of love enveloped him.

He couldn't face losing them. Either of them. Cody or Shelby.

His family.

What had made him think he could let either of them go? As Alex held onto the two most important people in his life, he knew he'd never voluntarily walk away from them again.

He could be a father. Not just because he loved them. But because he'd accepted the Lord. With God's love and guidance, he was certain he'd be a good father to Cody. And a faithful husband to Shelby.

If she'd have him.

"Stay strong, Shelby," he whispered, as the reassuring sounds of sirens filled the air. "Hang tight, my love. Help is on the way."

FIFTEEN

Alex was forced to move out of the way, placing Shelby's care in the hands of the paramedics once they arrived.

"Nice shot," Logan said, nudging Holden with his toe.

Alex shrugged, holding Cody against his shoulder and barely sparing his fellow DEA agent a glance. "I missed the first few times. God helped me in the end."

Logan raised a questioning brow. "You didn't miss," he said. "He was wearing body armor. I found three slugs, one in the chest, another one in the gut and the last one dead center in his head." He flashed a crooked grin. "Congratulations, I'd say you have your shooting arm back."

Alex simply shook his head. He knew that without the Lord's help, this night may have ended very differently. "Doesn't matter, I'm finished with the agency."

Logan looked surprised, but he didn't say anything.

After being treated for a minor injury on his right hand from one of Holden's wild shots, Russ Jacobson walked over. He eyed Alex suspiciously. "Did I hear my Grandson right? Did he call you daddy?"

Alex smoothed a hand down Cody's back and nodded. "Yes, sir. Cody is my son."

A fleeting expression of sorrow darkened the old man's

gaze. "Never did understand why Stephan and Trina acted the way they did, letting Cody stay all the time with Shelby. And there isn't a bit of Stephan in the boy."

The sight of the paramedics lifting Shelby onto a stretcher diverted Alex's gaze. "Excuse me," he muttered, before hurrying over. "Wait. Where are you taking her?"

"The closest hospital." The paramedic barely glanced at him, shoving Shelby inside the back of the ambulance and closing the door before Alex could try to jump in beside her.

"Come on," Russ came up to rest his hand on Alex's shoulder. "They're not going to let you and Cody ride along. I'll drive."

"McCade, where are you going?" Rafe asked testily from his seat near a second ambulance. He held an ice pack to the wound at his temple. "You can't leave until the scene has been cleared and all our statements have been given."

"They can come to the hospital to take my statement," Alex told them. "And I'm not with the agency any more, I quit."

Rafe and Logan gaped at him, as he followed Russ Jacobson to the church parking lot where he'd left his car.

Cody held tightly to Alex, as if he were afraid all the people he loved might leave him. He decided then and there to make another appointment with that child psychologist Shelby had found. Cody would need all the help and support he could get.

There was a strained silence in the car, as Shelby's father drove to the hospital.

"I'm sorry about Marilyn," Alex murmured.

Jacobson's mouth thinned and his expression was full of pain. "Thanks. Me, too. No matter what she was guilty of, she didn't deserve to die."

Alex winced, thinking about all the lives that had been lost. Trina, Bobby Drake and Marilyn. He prayed God would spare Shelby.

"So how long have you known about…" Russ Jacobson's voice trailed off as he glanced at his grandson.

"Not even a week," Alex said, not wanting to remind Cody of the night Trina had died.

"Hmm." Russ glanced at him. "And Shelby?"

Alex couldn't help but smile. "About the same time frame."

"So she's not seeing that coast guard guy?" Russ demanded.

"No, sir. Rafe was there to help protect her."

"From Holden?"

"From anyone who might want to hurt her." Alex frowned a bit. "I'm sorry to say, I suspected you might be in on the drug running operation."

Russ's mouth thinned. "I guess I can't blame you. I've been a fool. I discovered the drugs and was working closely with Holden to try to find out who was stashing them on my ships. I suspected Marilyn might be involved but Holden convinced me she was only hiding that she was fooling around with Bobby Drake. I never suspected he was the one behind the drugs all along."

"Don't feel bad, he had us fooled, as well," Alex said grimly. "He was Rafe's liaison inside the Green Bay police department. He had access to a lot of inside information."

Russ Jacobson pulled into the parking lot of the

hospital. He shut off the car and turned toward Alex. "What's your name, son?"

It felt strange to be considered this man's son, but he held Jacobson's gaze steadily with his. "Alex McCade. I used to be undercover for the DEA."

"But not any longer?" Jacobson asked.

"No. I love your daughter, sir. And if she'll have me, I promise to take good care of my family."

Russ Jacobson held out his hand and Alex took it. "I'll hold you to that promise," Jacobson warned. "My daughter and my grandson deserve the best."

"I know." Alex reached for the door handle, anxious to find out news about Shelby. "Let's go."

Once inside the hospital, they'd discovered Shelby had been taken straight to surgery. Alex finally convinced Cody to eat something, buying cheese and crackers from a nearby vending machine. When the doctor, who looked barely old enough to have finished medical school returned to the waiting room, Alex warily rose to his feet.

"Miss Jacobson's surgery went fine," he informed them. "We're going to watch her overnight in the ICU but only because the wound was so close to her spleen. We need to make sure she doesn't have any more bleeding. If all goes well, she'll be transferred to a regular room in the morning."

Alex closed his eyes on a wave of relief. "Thank You, Lord," he whispered.

"When can we see her?" Russ asked.

The young man glanced at his watch. "She'll be under the effects of anesthesia for about an hour or so. The nurses are getting her settled in the ICU as we speak. Generally visitors are limited to immediate family."

Alex opened his mouth to protest, but Jacobson beat him to it. "He is immediate family," he said in a firm tone. "And this boy is her son."

"No children," the doctor began but when he saw Russ's steely gaze, threw up his hands in defeat. "Just a quick visit then, no more than ten minutes."

"Thank you. We appreciate everything you've done," Alex said, smoothing things over.

"All in a day's work." The young surgeon shook both their hands and then left.

When they were finally allowed in the ICU, one glance at Shelby had Alex sucking in a harsh breath. She was hooked up to several IV pumps and a heart monitor was lit up above her bed. She looked so pale against the white sheets.

Holding Cody, he leaned over to take her hand, a lump forming in the back of his throat. "Shelby? Can you hear me?"

Her eyelids fluttered and she blinked, finally opening her eyes to look at them. "Cody?"

"He's right here," Alex said, holding Cody so she could see him. "See, Cody? I told you Aunt Shelby would be okay."

"I love you, Cody," she murmured, trying to smile.

"I love you, too." Cody's lower lip trembled. "Get better soon, okay?"

"I will." She glanced up at Alex. "Thank you."

He wasn't sure what she was thanking him for, and he leaned over to take her hand in his. "Shelby, everything is going to be fine. Holden is dead. He can't hurt anyone ever again."

She nodded, her eyelids fluttering closed.

The nurse hurried forward. "I'm sorry, but she really needs to rest. You'll have to come back in the morning."

Alex nodded and gently pulled his hand from her grasp. His eyes were suspiciously moist when he turned away.

"So, Cody, how would you like to come and stay with your grandpa tonight?" Russ asked when they'd left the ICU.

Cody tightened his grip on Alex's neck.

"If you don't mind, sir," Alex said. "I'd like to spend some quality time with my son."

Russ's smile was sad and Alex felt a little guilty, knowing the man was going home to an empty house. "Guess I can't blame you for that," Russ murmured.

Alex asked Russ to drop them off at the hotel, knowing that Rafe and Logan would know where to find him.

Exhausted, Cody protested going to sleep alone in his bed. Knowing the child had been through a lot, he kept Cody in his arms, as he sat back against the pillows on the bed.

And Alex found he didn't mind one bit, holding his son while the child slept.

Shelby's left side felt as if it were on fire. The doctors were pleased with her progress, though, explaining how lucky she'd been that they were able to save her spleen and that other than the blood she'd lost, she'd be fine.

"What does a spleen do, anyway?" she asked.

He launched into a lengthy explanation that quickly flew over her head. He'd ended the litany by explaining that without a spleen, she'd be on pills the rest of her life. She silently thanked God for sparing her life.

She was glad to be sent to a private room the following morning. From what she could tell, the other patients in the ICU were far worse off than she was.

Her father showed up early that morning. "Hi, Shelby," he greeted her, giving her a hug and a kiss. "I'm so glad you're doing better."

"Me, too." She smiled, determined to ignore the stabbing pain in her side.

"You must have been so frightened," he said, with a dark frown.

"Not really," she told him. "I know you never liked me to talk about my faith, but I wasn't afraid because I knew God was with me."

Her father stared down at her for a long moment. "You sound just like your mother when you say things like that."

"Mom?" Shelby was surprised. "I guess I do remember going to church with her, especially before she died."

Her father let out a heavy sigh. "I'm sorry, Shelby. I know I've been unfair with you, especially when you found strength in God. But your mother kept believing in God's love, right up until cancer stole her last breath."

Understanding dawned. "So that's why you didn't want to hear me talk about faith."

He hung his head. "I was wrong, I realize that now. I should have been smarter, but instead I made even more mistakes. Like marrying Marilyn. A woman who was helping Holden bring illegal drugs into the country on my ships."

She didn't know what to say to that, especially since she'd never liked Marilyn much. "It's not too late, Dad. God is always there, waiting for you."

He nodded slowly. "Maybe you're right. I think I'll

have a talk with the church pastor about it. But for now, I'd better get going. I have to make some arrangements for Marilyn's funeral."

"Do you have to?" She struggled to sit up. "Wait a few days, I'll help you. You shouldn't have to go through that alone."

"Relax, Shelby." He placed a reassuring hand on her shoulder, easing her back against the pillows. "I'm not mourning Marilyn, not in the way you're thinking. But I need to do this, to close this chapter of my life, once and for all."

"Oh." She felt bad for her father, but she was also impressed. He was handling the truth much better than she'd ever expected.

"Take care, Shelby. I'm sure your young man will bring Cody over to see you soon."

"I hope so. I miss him."

"Who? Your young man? Or Cody?"

She blushed, knowing she'd meant both. "Cody, of course. I'm sure he must be traumatized with everything that's happened."

"You're a good mother to Cody," he said. "The way you are with him, well, you remind me of your mother. In many ways. I love you, Shelby. I know I haven't always shown it, but I do."

"I know, Dad." She felt her eyes prick with tears. "I love you, too."

He left and she must have dozed because Alex gently shook her arm a short time later.

"Shelby? Wake up. Cody wants to say hi."

She shifted on the bed, wincing a bit when her stitches pulled. She focused on the tiny face peering at her from beside her bed. "I'm awake. Hey, partner. How are you?"

"Aunt Shelby!" Cody tried to climb up the side rails into her bed, holding one of the figures from his animal kingdom in one hand. Alex caught him under the arms, and swung him back down to the floor.

"Oh, no, you don't. You need to talk to her from here," he said, giving Cody a stern look.

"But, Dad," Cody protested.

"No buts," Alex interrupted. "You don't want to make her tummy hurt, do you?"

"No." Cody reluctantly gave in.

Shelby watched the two of them interact with a sense of shock. Cody had called Alex *Dad*. It seems they'd grown much closer in the time she'd been stuck in the hospital.

She swallowed hard, realizing God had brought father and son together. They didn't need her any more. She tried to quell the sense of panic.

"Shelby, are you really doing all right?" Alex glanced at her anxiously. "We've been so worried about you."

"I'm fine, really. And it seems you've been doing pretty well yourself."

"Me?" Alex's eyes widened. "I'm not the one lying in a hospital bed."

"No, but you've obviously spent time with Cody. He listens to you like a father." She hesitated, not wanting to bring up his career, but since they were talking about Cody's future, she steeled her resolve. "Have you thought about the future?"

"I already resigned from my job, Shelby. My boss has agreed to give me a reference so I can get a job in the training facility. You don't have to worry, I won't leave you and Cody alone."

Really? "You won't?"

"No." He glanced down at Cody who was trying to crawl under the bed. "I know this isn't the time, but you need to know, I'm not afraid to be a father to Cody. Not any more, although I was before. My own father, well, let's just say he wouldn't win any father-of-the-year awards."

She sucked in a quick breath. "Oh, Alex. He hit you?"

He shrugged and the way he avoided her gaze told her all she needed to know. "A bit, but he also drank. A lot. I've resented him for a long time. And I thought about giving up custody because I was a little afraid I'd turn out like he did."

Suddenly, everything made sense. She realized Alex wasn't avoiding being a father to Cody because he didn't love him, but because he didn't want to hurt him. "Oh, Alex. You'll be a great father to Cody." Her voice thickened with tears. "All he needs is love."

Alex nodded. "I know, because God showed me the way."

She couldn't have been happier to hear that.

"And what about you, Shelby?" he asked, gripping the edge of her side rail, tightly. "I know you've been afraid of men, but now that I've found you, I don't think I can let you go."

She blinked and the room spun dizzily. "I'm not afraid of you, Alex."

"You're sure?" He leaned over, reaching out to gently stroke her cheek. "Because if you need time, I can wait, for as long as it takes."

His offer was so sweet. "I'm sure, Alex. In those

brief moments I thought I might die, my biggest regret was not telling you how much I love you."

A broad smile bloomed on his face. "I love you, too, Shelby. Will you do me the honor of marrying me?"

Before she could formulate a response, the head of her bed moved upward and Alex reared back in surprise.

"What's going on?" she asked, fumbling for her controls. The foot of her bed began to rise up too, and for a moment she feared she might be a human sandwich. "Cody? Are you playing with the controls?"

His earnest face popped up from the other side of her bed. "My giraffe is stuck!"

Alex lunged to grab the toy wedged between the mattress and the controls of the bed rail. Her knees were almost to her chest and her head was raised up as high as it would go.

"Got it." He raised the toy, the expression on his face so similar to that of Cody's that silent laughter bubbled up inside her chest.

"Don't laugh, don't laugh," she moaned, holding her stomach tightly, even as her shoulders shook.

"Are you all right?" Alex asked anxiously as he pressed the buttons on her bed to put it back to normal. "Should I call the nurse for more pain medicine?"

"No, that's okay." She scrunched up her face but tears leaked out the corners of her eyes. She pulled herself together, taking a shaky breath. "Laughing hurts."

"I made the bed move." With the crisis over, Cody jumped up and down. "Did you see that? I made the bed move."

Alex scooped the boy into his arms, tickling him in the ribs. "You sure did, troublemaker, but you were supposed to be quiet for a few more minutes. At least until she'd given me an answer."

"What answer? What's the question?" Cody demanded.

Shelby gazed at them, her heart filled with joy and peace. The man she loved with her whole heart and the boy she loved like a son. "The answer is yes. Yes, I'll marry you."

"Did you hear that, Cody? We're going to be a family." Alex set Cody on his feet, gazing at Shelby with love in his eyes.

"Really?" Cody glanced at both of them. "A family that lives together?"

"Yes." Shelby reached out to take Alex's hand in hers, interlocking their fingers together. "A family that lives together, forever."

"Faith and love, Cody," Alex said softly, drawing Cody into their embrace. "All it takes is faith and love."

Shelby smiled through tears of happiness. "No fear."

* * * * *

Dear Reader,

I hope you enjoyed reading Alex and Shelby's story. As a mother, I know that I would do anything to protect my child and in this book Shelby must find Cody's biological father in order to keep her nephew safe even if that means she might lose custody of the child in the end. She loves Cody as if he was her own son, and throughout the story, Shelby prays to God for guidance and as always, He answers her prayers.

For Alex, this story is all about second chances. He made a mistake in the past, but has the opportunity now to make amends. Alex is more than willing to keep his son safe, but taking on the role of fatherhood is much more challenging.

Both Alex and Shelby must face their deepest fears, learning to put their faith and trust in God before they will find love and finally become united as a family.

I hope you enjoyed *Secret Agent Father*. I always enjoy hearing from my readers and I can be reached through my Web site at www.laurascottbooks.com.

Yours in faith,
Laura Scott

QUESTIONS FOR DISCUSSION

1. In the beginning of the story, Shelby has to make an impossible decision, to flee ensuring Cody's safety while leaving her seriously injured sister behind. Have you ever had to make a difficult decision and if so, how did you handle it?

2. Do you think Shelby does a good job of explaining to Cody about what Alex's role is in his life as his "other dad" or could she have handled this better?

3. In the early part of the book, Shelby is not very impressed with Alex's ability to be a good father to Cody. Do you think she is being unfair? Why or why not?

4. Alex doesn't have much experience with faith or believing in God, but at what point does he realize what he might be missing?

5. Shelby is more concerned about Cody's emotional health and his future, while Alex is more concerned with his son's immediate safety. Which should be the key priority and why?

6. Does Shelby do a good job of explaining heaven to Cody when he asks where his mother is? Why or why not?

7. Alex learns to pray when he's leading the way through the blizzard, knowing he must keep Shelby

and Cody safe. Discuss the circumstances in your life when you first learned to pray.

8. Shelby is determined to give Cody the chance to say goodbye to his mother at her funeral service. Did you agree with her decision? Why or why not?

9. One turning point in the story is when Alex decides to grant Shelby sole custody of Cody. Do you think he is really making this decision based on what's best for Cody? Why or why not?

10. At what point in the story does Shelby fully embrace her faith in the Lord? Have you ever had a similar experience?

11. How does Alex use his newfound faith to save Shelby's life?

12. Both Shelby and Alex must face their respective fears. Discuss a point in your life when you used your faith in God to face your fears.

Here's a sneak preview of
THE RANCHER'S PROMISE by Jillian Hart
Available in June 2010 from Love Inspired

"So, are you back to stay?" Justin's deep voice hid any shades of emotion. Was he fishing for information or was he finally about to say "I told you so"?

"I'll probably go back to teaching in Dallas, but things could change. I'll just have to wait and see." The things in life she used to think were so important no longer mattered. Standing on her own two feet, building a life for herself, healing her wounds—that did.

"And this man you married?" he asked. "Did he leave you or did you leave him?"

"He threw me out." She waited for Justin's reaction. Surely a man with that severe a frown on his face was about to take delight in the irony. She'd turned down Justin's love, and her husband of five years had thrown away hers. If she were Justin, she would want her off his land.

"You were nothing but honest with me back then." He leaned against the railing, the wind raking his dark hair, and a different emotion passed across his hard countenance. "I was the one who never listened. I loved you so much, I don't think I could hear anything but what I wanted."

"I loved you, too. I wish I could have been different for you." Helpless, she took another step toward the driveway. She didn't know how to thank him. He could be treating her a lot worse right now, and she would deserve it. "Goodbye, Justin."

"I suppose you need a job?"

"I'll figure out something." Need a job? No, she was frantic for one. How did she tell him the truth?

Find out in THE RANCHER'S PROMISE
Available June 2010 from Love Inspired

Love Inspired

Bestselling author

JILLIAN HART

brings you another heartwarming story
from

the
GRANGER
FAMILY
RANCH

Rancher Justin Granger hasn't seen his high school sweetheart
since she rode out of town with his heart. Now she's back, with
sadness in her eyes, seeking a job as his cook and housekeeper.
He agrees but is determined to avoid her...until he discovers
that her big dream has always been him!

The Rancher's Promise

*Available June
wherever books are sold.*

Love Inspired
SUSPENSE

TITLES AVAILABLE NEXT MONTH

Available June 8, 2010

END GAME
Big Sky Secrets
Roxanne Rustand

RISKY REUNION
Protecting the Witnesses
Lenora Worth

TROUBLED WATERS
Rachelle McCalla

SABOTAGE
Kit Wilkinson

LISCNMBPA0510